MRS. VARGAS
◇ AND DEAD
THE
NATURALIST

MRS. VARGAS ◇ AND THE DEAD NATURALIST

By

KATHLEEN ALCALÁ

K. Alcalá
December 4,
1992

CALYX BOOKS
CORVALLIS • OREGON

The publication of this book was supported with grants from the National Endowment for the Arts, the Oregon Arts Commission, and the King County Arts Commission.

Cover art, *Nuestra Señora de la Selva*, by Alfredo Arreguin
Cover design by Carolyn Sawtelle and Cheryl McLean
Book design by Cheryl McLean

CALYX Books are distributed to the trade through major library distributors, jobbers, and most small press distributors including: Airlift, Bookpeople, Bookslinger, Inland Book Co., Pacific Pipeline, and Small Press Distribution. For personal orders or other information write: CALYX Books, PO Box B, Corvallis, OR 97339, (503) 753-9384.

∞
The paper in this book meets the guidelines for permanence and durability of the Committee on Production Guidelines for Book Longevity of the Council on Library Resources and the minimum requirements of the American National Standard for the Permanence of Paper for Printed Library Materials Z38.48-1984.

Library of Congress Cataloging-in-Publication Data

Alcalá, Kathleen J., 1954 -
    Mrs. Vargas and the dead naturalist / Kathleen J. Alcalá.
        p.   cm.
    ISBN 0-934971-26-9 (alk.paper) : $18.95. — ISBN 0-934971-25-0 (pbk. : alk. paper) : $9.95.
    1. Mexican American women—Fiction. 2. Women—Mexico—Fiction. I. Title.
PS3551.L287M77   1992
813'.54—dc20   92-4469
                                                  CIP

Printed in the U.S.A.

ACKNOWLEDGEMENTS

The author gratefully acknowledges The King County Arts Commission, the Cottages at Hedgebrook, and Artist Trust for enabling her to complete this project.

She also acknowledges the following publications in which these stories were previously published in slightly different form: "Mrs. Vargas and the Dead Naturalist," *The Seattle Review*, Vol. VIII, No. 2, 1985; "Taking Inventory," *The Daily*, University of Washington, February 5, 1986; "Amalia," *Women and Aging* (CALYX Books, 1986); "Reflection in the Eye of a Crow," *Black Ice*, Vol. 3, 1987; "The Transforming Eye," CALYX, *A Journal of Art and Literature by Women*, Vol. 12, No. 2, 1989; "The Fire of San Marcos," *Chiricú*, Vol. 5, No. 2, 1989; "Sweetheart," *Isaac Asimov's Magazine of Fantasy and Science Fiction*, Davis Publications, Inc., Vol. 15, No. 3, March 1991; "Flora's Complaint," *Magic Realism by Women—Dreams in a Minor Key* (Crossing Press, April 1991) edited by Susanna J. Sturgis.

With special thanks to Wayne and Benjamín.
This book is dedicated to the memory of my
Aunt Rosa Fe Narro Arrien, with love.

CONTENTS

PREFACE

T here is a garden surrounded by a crumbling
stucco wall where the flowers always bloom and
the sound of running water is incessant. There is no
time and all time. Cool shadows fall across the warmth
of the courtyard, a late afternoon in late summer, a time
for remembering. The people who wander through this
garden—a bruja, an ugly young woman, and a woman as
gracious to dead guests as live ones—find it is time to
move on to another form of existence; for others, it is
time to take control of the lives they have. Miracles
flower in this neglected courtyard, and old women grapple
with the devil or converse with angels. A priest seeks
immortality through the smell of beauty, and the under-
taker misses his own cue.

Like the Mexican writer Elena Poniatowska, I have
tried to tell the stories my characters would tell if they
were writers. Many of the stories concern the women
who came of age in the United States within a Mexican
social structure, surrounded by a pre-Columbian landscape and sensibility. I owe a special debt to Juan Rulfo,
the Mexican writer who gave voice to the blood-soaked
earth of the Mexican Revolution and portrayed a people
who endure. "La Esmeralda," the final story, goes back a

little farther in time to people already buffeted by the forces that will tear the country apart fifty years later.

These stories are about inner landscapes; they explore the invisible world behind the visible, and the characters who move in both worlds through the windows of dream and imagination.

This is the "interior" West that must accompany the exterior one, the cactus and gunsmoke reflected in an obsidian mirror. When the reader looks in that mirror, I expect her to see a room not the room in which she stands, a hint of roses in the air, or is it copal? the sound of the ocean that must be thousands of miles away, a piano, an empty cradle... where is the pianist? where is the baby? there are so many stories to tell....

K. Alcalá
Seattle, Washington
January 1992

THE TRANSFORMING EYE

T here were Japanese fishing floats and a dried wreath of grape vines, Persian boxes with enamelled gazelles on the lids, rubber stamps of business addresses, broken coffee mugs, dog leashes, and partially disassembled clocks. Through the window, I could just see either a fur coat or a stuffed animal, several war medals, and some worn leather gloves in a corner; an aviator's cap, drafting tools, and a tied bundle of old fountain pens; tiny dolls with amazed expressions on their faces, accompanied by a straw man on a burro; a saddle with silver trimming, and four matching teacups and saucers. A dried porcupine fish hung from the ceiling, and several transparent, dried seahorses crumbled on the ledge in the late afternoon sunlight. Volumes of books with illegible titles, a lace collar, a scattering of hatpins, and a string of pearls spilled off the shelf below the window.

Each item, I felt sure, had a reason for being there; each had a story of mystery and romance. There, I thought, is what's missing from Los Picos. "The Transforming Eye" was lettered on the glass, and below that "Fine Photography—a Gift to Last Forever" in fancy gold script. It appeared to be more of an antique store than a photographer's studio. A symbol in gold—an eye peering between the legs of a camera tripod—completed the dusty window. Except for the light from the street, all was dark inside, and gave the illusion of a half-opened trunk discovered in an attic, filled with lost items from the past. The street remained empty, the shadows long, and I returned home accompanied only by my own footsteps.

◇ ◇ ◇

I came to Los Picos to help my grandmother to die. My ancient great-aunts, Doña Luisa and Doña Elvira, could no longer care for Abuelita Clara, my grandmother, who lay curled like a mummified doll in her giant mahogany bed. I was between jobs as a television production assistant when they invited me down. Who could refuse an all-expense paid summer in Mexico, even if it was in a small town?

My great-aunts, although well into their seventies, continued with their business of making fine linens. The two no longer did the fine needlework themselves, but hired young women with keen eyesight and strong fingers. The hired women worked in a room which had originally been the parlor, and sometimes one or the other of my great-aunts would sit down at the monstrous sewing machine to hem a finished tablecloth if an order were running late. A renewed interest in fine, hand-made items had made my great-aunts well off, and they moved with the grace and assurance of the financially and socially secure.

I fed Abuelita and read to her in the mornings, then tried to feed her again at noon, coaxing a few warm noodles between her slack lips. Her dentures lay on the nightstand, unused. The room smelled of glycerin and rosewater, and the stale, sharp smell of old people. Sometimes a tear rolled down my grandmother's cheek, and I didn't know if it was the story I was reading or if she was thinking of something sad. We were said to resemble each other, with our high cheekbones and curly hair, and I watched her palsied hands and trembling lip as though contemplating my own future.

In the afternoons she slept, and I walked slowly up and down the narrow, cobblestoned streets of Los Picos, nodding to the shopkeepers, the flower vendor, and the young woman who cared for the children in the corner house. I saw the same people every day. On the Calle Benito Juarez, which ran all the way around the plaza, was a magazine stand that carried an English language paper; sometimes I read it. The news seemed strange and distant.

In the evenings, we wrapped my grandmother in shawls and carried her out to the front room, where the sewing machine stood in its canvas cover like a horse in its stall, and we sat and read or talked. We thought the change of scene might cheer Abuelita up, and it was easier to talk to her if there were others in the room who could answer. We propped her up in an overstuffed chair, and she stared at us with great brown owl eyes, magnified by her ill-fitting glasses.

"What did you do today?" asked Doña Luisa, rattling a sheaf of papers as she did her accounts for the day.

"I walked way down there," I said, mimicking my aunts in my exaggeration, "and way, way up a steep hill, so steep I thought I would fall off backwards."

"Oh!" said Doña Elvira. "How tiring! I don't like to walk up those hills."

"What was the name of the street you were on?" asked Luisa.

"I don't remember," I said. "I forgot to look. But there was some kind of a shop up there, like a photographer's shop. It was called 'The Transforming Eye.'"

"I don't know what that could be," said Luisa. "I haven't been up that way in ages."

"There used to be that crazy Dutchman," said Elvira. "He had an art studio, or something."

"Oh, him!" said Luisa, dismissing the idea with her hand. "He was always arguing with people and filling their heads with strange ideas... Hoove, or Noobes. They ran him out of Europe for being an anarchist or Mason or some such nonsense."

"He sounds interesting," I said.

"No, no. Well, maybe to you," said Luisa, "but he died a long time ago. There used to be people like that all over Mexico, in exile."

"Like Trotsky," said Elvira. "Did Noobes really die?"

"I suppose so," said Luisa. "Who's heard anything of him in ages? Anyway, he was just trouble."

"Too bad," said Elvira, "he was very handsome. He had his eye on your grandmother."

"Yes, but she would have none of it," added Luisa quickly. "She was already engaged to your grandfather."

"Really?" I asked.

"Yes, but enough of that," said Luisa. "Sometimes the past is best forgotten. It's time for bed."

I slept in an enclosed porch off the parlor, surrounded by the spools of colored thread with which the women worked during the day. The vivid magentas and greens and golds seemed to embody the fantastic designs into which they would one day be transformed, and I could sense their glowing presence in the dark.

It rained every day for the next week. The deep gray clouds piled up and piled up until the mountaintops could hold them no longer, then sheets of rain would come crashing down on the town. Each day, the rain came as a relief, the temperature and humidity remaining high until the clouds burst. Our clothes stuck to us, and my aunts carried handkerchiefs soaked in perfume to dab at their brows as they worked. In the courtyard, the doves huddled and cooed, as though mourning their children which were just the right age to be baked into delicious little pies.

On Friday, the sky was white and opaque, but it did not rain. I went for my first walk in five days, heading east along the near edge of the plaza, then up into the streets on that side of town. The weather turned suddenly, and it began to rain in fat, wet drops. I headed for a worn green awning, and found myself back in front of The Transforming Eye. The front door stood open, so I stepped into the dark, woody-smelling interior.

The shop sagged with dust and neglect. Stacks of old photographs lay in the corners, dismembered frames, and old ends of cardboard. A counter stood opposite the door, but was piled so high with musty books and papers that it was obviously not used for business. A man bending over an old camera looked up at me. He had dark eyes and light, greying hair, and looked somewhere between forty and fifty years old.

"Hello," I said.

"Hello," he grunted, and bent back over the camera. I stood there for several moments before he looked back at me, as though surprised to see a real person in his shop.

"I just came in from the rain," I said, "and was enjoying the things in your shop. Some of them are very old."

"My father's things," he said.

"This is your father's shop?" I asked, and began thumbing through the stacks of old photos. The pictures were striking, and the people seemed very life-like in spite of their stiff poses and formal clothes. Beyond the photos were glass plates covered with dust.

"Was," he answered.

I walked further into the shop and found an area arranged for portraits. There were old hats, sprays of artificial flowers, and what looked like everybody's family Bible. Behind was a painted backdrop. It was in fantastic colors with a checkerboard floor in the foreground.

"This is beautiful!" I exclaimed. The backdrop was Moorish in style, and showed an impossibly lush scene of bright trees and flowers, with mysterious red minarets in the background. Near the center, two lime-green parrots shared a hoop and touched bills affectionately, framed by a full moon. The black and white checkerboard pattern appeared to recede into the trees and buildings above it.

I made my way back to the front of the store and repeated myself: "The backdrop is very beautiful."

"Yes," he said, looking at me. "It came from the cargo of a Portuguese shipwreck. It is very old."

"It looks it," I said, then watched his deft hands as he worked on the camera. I found myself fascinated by his movements and his clothes. He wore a white shirt with the sleeves rolled up, high-waisted trousers, and a vest with a gold chain dangling from the watch pocket. It had stopped raining outside, and was very bright in contrast to the gloomy interior of the shop.

"There," he said, standing back from the camera.

"Do you know how to use it?" I asked.

"My father taught me before I left. But it needs glass plates. It doesn't use film."

"I saw some glass back there," I said, "behind the counter."

He looked at me more carefully as I stood with my hand on the door, ready to leave. "Maybe I'll have the camera working by next week."

That evening I teased my great-aunts. "I found that crazy Dutchman."

"How could you?" asked Elvira. "He's long gone."

"Not really. It was his son. He was trying to fix an old camera. And there's a beautiful backdrop for picture-taking!"

"Really!" said Luisa. "Well, you be careful up there. His father was involved in sorcery, or some such trash. That's why his wife left him."

"Oh, I think I'll be all right," I said. "He doesn't seem to know much about his father's business, much less any sorcery."

Abuelita Clara's face contorted with pain or discomfort, so we carried her back to her room and laid her in the embrace of the great mahogany bed.

I dreamed that night about the backdrop. In it, dusty photos were piled on the checkerboard foreground, and the fountains were running with ice-blue water. When I awoke, it was raining again.

When a week and a day had passed, I returned to The Transforming Eye. The door was open, and a few cobwebs had been cleared away. The photographer was peering at the exotic backdrop through the lens of the old camera.

"I think it's working," he said, "but I'm having trouble adjusting the angle. It seems to slip. There are some prints I've developed," he said nodding to the counter. "I keep getting things in the frame that don't belong. I've cleared out some of this stuff, so that should help."

One print showed the backdrop with a stuffed pheasant in the foreground. Another showed a large plumed hat on a stone bench, as though left by a distracted lady to be picked up in a moment. I looked around the shop and saw neither of these objects.

"These are in black and white," I said, disappointed. "The colors of the backdrop don't show."

"No," he said, "but they can be colored by hand." He stooped and peered through the camera lens.

"Can you do that?"

"Yes," he said. "My father taught me the craft when I was little. I often colored his prints for him, although he never told the customers."

After another silence, he said, "Come sit over here. I need a human subject. That way I can tell if it really works or not."

I sat in a rickety chair before the backdrop, which glowed with jewel-like colors, while the photographer arranged the lights. When he told me to look up, I did, and sat very still while he exposed the plate.

During that time he said, "Your eyes are very lovely. They remind me of a woman my father used to know."

I could feel my cheeks grow warm under the compliment, although I could not speak. The photographer looked younger than the first time I had seen him.

At last he said, "That's it. You're finished," and I jumped up, almost knocking the chair into the backdrop.

"Now," he said, smiling and placing a hand lightly on my shoulder, "come back next week and I'll have the photo ready. If it's good I'll even color it and give you the print."

"I would like that," I said. "It will give me something by which to remember Los Picos."

He laughed and said, "Why would anyone want to remember Los Picos?"

I smiled and said goodbye. Passing the open door, I noticed that it said in small gold letters, "Hiram Noobes & Son." My feet flew down the cobblestoned streets as I tried to escape the afternoon rainstorm, but I still returned to my aunts' house slightly damp.

"I just had my picture taken," I announced gaily to Elvira when she opened the door for me.

She looked at me slowly and said, "By whom?"

"By Hiram Noobes' son, the photographer."

At the mention of that name, Elvira and Luisa, who had entered the front hall to see who was at the door, stopped where they were.

"You must not go there anymore!" said Luisa finally.

"But why?" I asked, confused by their reaction. I thought they might be pleased by an old-fashioned photograph.

"Some of his father's friends disappeared. No one knows what happened to them," said Luisa.

"Well, you said he was an anarchist," I answered. "Maybe they went to start revolutions in other countries. I don't understand why you're so upset."

"A photograph can possess a person's soul," said Elvira quietly.

I almost burst out laughing. "No one believes that except a few old Indians in the hills!"

"That's enough!" said Luisa, so I went to get my grandmother ready for dinner. I felt sorry for myself, young in a house full of old women, and thought it was just as well that I would be returning to California soon to start a new project.

Dinner was very quiet that night. No one had much of an appetite, and we all retired early to our rooms. My aunts' stories had made me all the more curious about the handsome photographer, but at the same time, I felt that it was time to leave. I tried to book an earlier flight out of Guadalajara the next day, but the airlines couldn't accommodate me. I fed bread crumbs to the doves in the courtyard and shared their mournful mood.

I decided to confide in my grandmother. Although she no longer spoke, I thought that she might have some sympathy. For all I knew, she might have been prevented from marrying Noobes by custom and family politics. As I spoke, her eyes grew rounder and rounder behind her thick glasses.

Finally, she pulled me towards her with a claw-like hand and rasped, with great effort, "Go back. Go back to Los Angeles."

Tears started to my eyes. She, too, had grown tired of me. I ran from her room and spent the rest of the afternoon locked in the little enclosed porch, looking through a book which I had no heart to read.

When I returned to The Transforming Eye, I hurried inside, more anxious to see him than I had realized. The photographer was not there. I paced about nervously, thinking that he must have stepped out for a moment, since the door had been left ajar.

Several new prints lay on a corner of the worn marble counter. They showed a serious young woman holding a bowl of pomegranates in her lap. One of the prints had been tinted. I admired the life-like quality of the photos, until I realized that the woman in the picture was me. The stiff pose and the artificial coloring made me look like someone I recognized, but not like me.

What was even more puzzling was that I had not been holding a bowl of pomegranates when the portrait was taken. He must have drawn it in, although the bowl appeared in all six prints, and he would have had to redraw my hands to make the change.

Impatient, I stepped back into the portrait area to see if the photographer was there. The lights were on, and the backdrop glowed enticingly. On the stone bench in the scene was a wooden bowl full of deliciously red pomegranates. They looked so real that I couldn't restrain myself from reaching to pick one up. The leathery skin and prickly end felt as real to me as any fruit I had ever touched. I turned with the pomegranate in my hand and saw that I stood on the black and white tiles, the bright trees trailing their branches over my head. The photographer's studio appeared vague and dim, as though seen through a gauze curtain. I was inside the backdrop. When I tried to step out, I was restrained by an invisible barrier, which gave slightly and sprang back at my touch.

Convinced that this was some sort of illusion, I sat down on the stone bench and resolved not to panic. I would wait for the photographer to return, enjoy his prank, and free me. Maybe then he would take me out to lunch.

In time, the photographer returned, looking as distant and self-absorbed as ever, and didn't seem to notice that anything was different. He acted as though he didn't see me.

"Hey!" I said finally. "Noobes! Are you through? I'm getting bored in here." And I tried to laugh. He still didn't seem to notice. "Hey!" I yelled, beating my hands against the invisible restraint. "Let me out now!"

Noobes sat by the front window sorting tools. He checked his pocket watch once, then returned to turn off the lights. When he did, it became night in the backdrop.

"No!" I screamed. "Don't leave me here!"

I heard the door shut and lock.

I screamed and clawed at the barrier until I was hoarse and my hands raw and bleeding, but I could not cut my way out. Tears coursed down my face and neck, but I didn't stop to wipe them away until much later. Exhausted, I sank back onto the cold tiles, still sobbing. When I was finally silent, I realized that I could hear the fountain splashing, and a faint breeze stirred the palm trees, bringing the scent of night-blooming jasmine.

It seemed like a long time that I was trapped in the backdrop. The mountains were painted onto another invisible barrier, so there was no more depth in there, at least not for me, than was visible from outside. Sometimes I would see others, men in turbans with swords at their waists, and women in long lace dresses, people from the near past and long ago, but they did not come near. Once, a man seemed to step closer and look at me, but after a minute he went away. Birds sang constantly, and roses and gardenias bloomed in the hidden courtyards. I ate two of the pomegranates.

I found my grandmother's handkerchief in the backdrop, embroidered with her initials in my aunts' distinctive style. I was holding it in one hand and trailing the other in the ice-cold waters of the fountain when a pinpoint of light seemed to open up before me. I stood up and could see my grandmother walking towards me, under her own power. I threw myself in her arms, and she held me in a strong embrace before stepping past me to the fountain, and I saw a man with light hair and dark eyes coming towards her. Just before I found myself back in the shop, I saw that my grandmother looked like the tinted photograph of myself as she reached out her hand to Hiram Noobes.

◇ ◇ ◇

I returned to the house of my great-aunts to find that my grandmother had died. It was late evening of the same day, and while my aunts had been worried about me, they were too distraught to question me closely. They did not see my tear-streaked face and bloody hands through their own grief.

I don't remember much of what happened during the following days. My aunts were like darkness, pulled into themselves, nursing their grief behind shawls.

Women I had not seen before prepared my grandmother's body for burial, perfuming it and painting her face with cosmetics. I could not help but think that they could never make her look as beautiful as the last glimpse I had of her retreating into that gauze-veiled garden of dreams.

I felt useless. There was no place for me in this atmosphere of ritual grief. I had wept all my tears into the ice-blue fountain, and had none left for my Abuela as the coffin was lowered into the grave in the cramped hillside cemetery. I wore a borrowed rebozo over my head and shoulders since I had lacked the foresight to bring mourning clothes to Los Picos.

Immediately after the funeral, I took the bus to Guadalajara from where my airplane would depart that evening. My aunts had been subdued and distant—I could not read their careworn faces as they kissed me goodbye. I knew that I could never ask them the many questions that I had about The Transforming Eye.

As the bus topped the last rise from which the town of Los Picos was visible, I thought I saw a golden glimmer from a distant hillside, afternoon sunlight glinting off a plate glass window with gold lettering, a gift to last forever.... Or maybe I just imagined it. I hid my battered fingernails in my grandmother's handkerchief and refused to look back again.

I never went to see my great-aunts again, though I think of them when I spread my embroidered tablecloth for special dinners, and I hope that my grandmother is happy, wherever she is, inside of The Transforming Eye.

SWEETHEART

When people noticed Corazón, it was to say "She certainly doesn't resemble her sister."

Corazón was tall and shy. At seventeen, she had never had a boyfriend, and felt that her overly romantic name, which meant "sweetheart," mocked her. With her height and frizzy hair, Corazón looked like a dark candle standing at the back in her senior class picture, her mournful gaze lost in the reflection off her glasses.

Corazón's younger sister was named Isabella, called Queenie. Where Corazón was shy, Queenie could captivate a group with her quick wit and flirtatious personality. If Queenie could have helped it, no one in San Antonio would have known that they were sisters at all.

Corazón worked in a place called Dixie's Burgers. When she graduated from high school, no one asked if she had any further plans. Each day she walked to work with the hot Texas sky pressed down upon her, and tied on a butterscotch-colored apron before taking her place behind the counter.

That was the summer that Arturo and Tonia's son came home on leave. Art Junior served in the Merchant Marine. Although he was short like his father, his life at sea gave him a self-confidence no job in San Antonio could have offered. Soon he had a following of neighborhood boys gathered every time he stopped in the diner to tell one of his stories.

Art had been to Hong Kong and India, to the Philippines and Singapore, everywhere a ship could travel, and as he told about meeting Russian sailors and Japanese fishermen, he would hold his audience rapt with his level gray gaze. Even Corazón would pause from cleaning the counter as Art talked, while the flies buzzed and steam condensed around the fluorescent lights on the ceiling.

"So then this good-looking Jap girl comes out and bows to you. She's wearing this kimono and these sandals that make it so she can hardly walk. You bow, and she hands you a flower. A girl gives a guy a flower. Then everyone bows again and sits on the floor and she serves you tea. That's all there is to it."

Corazón thought about the tea ceremony for a long time afterwards. That night, she imagined herself handing a perfect flower, a chrysanthemum, to a man. She could not see his face, but he had fine, artistic hands. "Thank you," he said, and she fell asleep.

When Art came into Dixie's Burgers to tell his stories, Corazón tried to creep closer so that she could hear without being seen. Not that he would have noticed. Every girl in the neighborhood was trying to get his attention, but Art and Queenie hit it off right away. Although her parents thought she was too young to have a novio, Queenie and Art spent a lot of time together, hanging around Dixie's and the riverfront.

Art mostly told stories about the good times he and his buddies had in different ports, but sometimes he talked about how hard life at sea was, and the mysterious things that could happen there. Corazón began to imagine herself as an invisible passenger on a ship like his, the *U.S.S. Adventurer*, free to move about the decks, walkways, and passages without being observed, watching the sailors do their jobs, and visiting strange and exotic ports with them.

After each time that Art came into Dixie's and told a story, Corazón would repeat it to herself while falling asleep that night. She could almost feel the gentle rise and fall of the ship under her as she dozed off. After awhile, she was keeping an invisible journal and sending postcards to invisible relatives. She imagined herself dressed in a long, pale pink coat with a large-brimmed hat and a long trailing scarf around her neck. Corazón practiced her handwriting to give it just the right flourish.

My dearest Hermalinda,

The weather is lovely in Kuala Lumpur. The monsoons have not yet begun, but the orchid forests are in full bloom. I do hope little Josie is over the chicken pox.

Yours faithfully,
Corazón

Art told a story about stopping in the Aleutian Islands, and Corazón stood on the deck in a fur wrap as the ship glided past huge, unfathomably blue glaciers. Eskimos came out to greet them in kayaks.

Later, after traveling through perilous seas, the ship docked briefly in Hawaii, and Corazón waved a fond farewell as the perfume from the many leis around her neck filled the air around her.

My Dear Tía Rosauria, (she wrote)

The Pacific seas are endlessly blue. Dolphins follow us for miles, as though fascinated by this huge, floating city. We are headed for the South Pacific, where palm trees sway in balmy breezes.

Sorry to miss the garden party this year. Please convey my regrets to Uncle.

Fondly,
Corazón

Corazón's ship-going alter ego had by now abandoned her flowing pink coat for the more practical bell-bottoms of the sailors, and even enjoyed their singing in the evenings. She wore a navy peacoat against the evening chill, and read her mail as eagerly as the young men who suffered from being so far from home. Sometimes she had a fiancé who played polo in Argentina, but when she tired of his endless chatter about horses, Corazón fancied a minor count in a small European country. They both remained vague, distant figures, and Corazón felt no compulsion to cut her voyage short and return to either of them. As she scrubbed down the metal counters at Dixie's or sprayed stain-remover on her greasy uniform before washing it, Corazón composed letters in her head to her two beaus, scarcely noticing the heat and grime that were a constant part of her life.

By early August, Art's leave was almost over. He and Queenie seemed to slip away more and more often, and Corazón suspected that her sister was sneaking out at night to see him. His appearances at Dixie's were less frequent, but his stories seemed to be taking a more fantastic turn. Corazón suspected that he had run out of real stories, and was starting to make things up just to please the hungry faces around him. She didn't mind. The more exotic his voyages, the more wonderful her own.

One especially oppressive afternoon, when the dogs lay in the dust in any patch of shade and the little old ladies didn't even bother to move their chairs outside, Art swung into Dixie's for a cold beer. He seemed unusually pensive and took a plastic straw out of the dispenser to chew on. Five neighborhood boys soon surrounded him and took chairs at the little tables nearby.

"Tell us about monsters," said Jorge. "Didn't you see any sea monsters out there?"

Art thought about this as he sprawled in his chair. "Yeah," he said, "I seen some pretty strange things. Not monsters, exactly. More like weird fish. Though not really fish." His eyes narrowed as he thought. "I guess they was mermaids."

A general sound of disbelief rose from the group.

"Aw, c'mon," said Jorge. "You didn't see no mermaids. There's no such thing!"

"Well," said Art. "I'll tell you exactly what happened, and you can make up your own minds. I'm not saying I did, and I'm not saying I didn't, but something strange was going on out there. I'm not the only one who saw it. A bunch of the guys did."

Corazón moved down the counter in order to hear better.

"We was way down in the Indian Ocean, near a bunch of islands called the Maldives. We was a little off course, though the navigator wouldn't admit it until we came right up to these islands he didn't know was there."

Art squirmed down in his seat as he talked, and seemed to be in a more serious mood than usual. His audience waited quietly, sipping their Cokes and wiping their sweaty hands on their jeans.

"There are coral reefs out there, so we decided to stop until we could figure out where we was. We dropped anchor in a bay between two islands, and you could hear the howler monkeys calling back and forth between the trees. The water was dead calm, and you could see clear to the bottom. We was all out on deck smoking and stuff, but outside of the howlers, it was real quiet, kind of eerie.

"Jim, Slim Jim, we call him, was bragging about his girlfriend, who's an Olympic swimmer or something, when one of the guys points in the water and says, 'Hey Jim, there goes your girlfriend now!' We all started laughing, figuring it was some fat porpoise or even a cowfish, these really ugly things, but it was something I'd never seen before, real human-like. It was circling the ship about a hundred yards away, and the light was getting dim, so it was hard to see. Kind of brown and shiny. We'd about decided it was a big sand shark, or some other reef fish, when there's this sharp whistle from near one of the islands. This thing we'd been watching raises up out of the water and lets out a really sharp whistle in return, like an answer. It looked just like a woman when it did that, with long hair and big boobs and everything."

Art sounded so serious at this point that the boys didn't even snicker. Corazón stood transfixed at the counter, not even pretending not to listen.

"Well, after that," said Art, still chewing on the straw, "we got out a spotlight and tried to see it better, but by then it was gone. The sun had gone down, and the captain refused permission for a small boat to go out. All we could do was wonder what the hell it was all about.

"The next day, we got our bearings and headed up to Sri Lanka. We'd been south of where we were supposed to be, and the captain was pretty pissed. Anyway, we got an afternoon's leave in Sri Lanka, which is on a big island near India, and some of us got to talking to some shipping clerks who spoke English. We described what we'd seen the night before. One of the Sri Lankans said there was legends about warrior mermaids in those waters. He said there are abandoned temples, and the mermaids are guardian spirits. They kill men who try to go ashore. The other Sri Lankans looked real uncomfortable, because they don't want us to think they're superstitious. They wouldn't let the other guy talk anymore, so we left."

Art sat quiet for a moment, then sat up and said, "That's it. That's my mermaid story. You guys don't believe it, suit yourselves."

"I don't believe it," said Manny. "You're just pulling our leg."

"I wouldn't do that," said Art, standing up. "I wouldn't do that!"

He grabbed Manny by the leg and dragged him out of the chair kicking and hollering until the boss, Nelson, came out and told them to cut the rough stuff. Then they all went outside, leaving Corazón glued to the counter by her greasy rag until Nelson told her to get back to work. She hurried out to clean up their table and found a small, rough pebble where Art had sat. Without thinking, Corazón slipped it into her pocket before picking up the plastic cups and running her damp rag across the tabletop.

That night, Corazón dreamed again of the rise and fall of the waves. But this time, she was in the waves, not on them. She felt her long green hair as it trailed about her neck and shoulders, and felt the little fish that moved under her hands and brushed her sides as she swam. When she rose out of the water on her tail, she could just glimpse a crumbling white temple through the trees of the island. A piercing whistle startled her awake, but it was only the alarm clock saying it was time to get up.

Corazón stumbled to the bathroom, where she was disappointed by her short, lifeless hair and flat chest. No warrior mermaid wore glasses, only a waitress at Dixie's in San Antonio. She threw down her glasses and got in the shower to disperse the night's dreams.

Corazón stopped being a passenger on the ship, and scarcely listened to Art's stories when he came in now. As the end of his leave approached, he spent less time in Dixie's, and Corazón figured he was spending more time with Queenie.

Corazón stopped writing to the aunt and uncle in San Francisco, and gave up on the polo player and the European playboy. She laid the imaginary pink dress and coat in a steamer trunk, and carefully wrapped the wide-brimmed hat in tissue paper before placing it in a leather hatbox. Then she shed her clothes and jumped overboard into the still green waters of the lagoon. She found a copper spear lying on the white sand, green with age, and carried it as lightly as a cane. It fit her hand exactly.

"I'm going to have to let you go if you don't shape up," said Nelson. "You've been daydreaming an awful lot lately. There're plenty more would like your job if you don't."

Corazón promised to pay more attention. But the bright Texas sunlight hurt her eyes now, and she longed for the watery depths of sleep. She moved clumsily about the diner, thrashing at glasses as though they were always out of reach, dropping the plastic trays when she tried to stack them on the counter. Only at night did she move gracefully, the warm waters like a mantle across her shoulders, the whistling language ringing in her ears.

The day before his leave ended, Art stopped in at Dixie's to say goodbye to the boys. There was a lot of kidding around and punching, and Corazón went to the back room to get supplies and escape the noise. As she pushed the swinging door to return, Corazón heard one of the boys ask Art if he really had seen a mermaid.

"Yeah, a beaut," said Art. "A real sailor's dream. And you know what I'd do if I caught one?"

Here, Art suggested something that couldn't possibly be done to a mermaid, twisting his thumb low in the air before him as he said it. The boys giggled wickedly, if a little uncertainly, and Corazón sagged against the door, unable to go either out front or back. She realized at that moment, as though she had been struck in the face, that Art had done this to her sister Queenie. All the blood rose to her head, then drained away. She dropped the plastic plates and paper napkins on the floor. Corazón turned dully when footsteps approached.

"What's the matter?" asked Nelson. "You look awful."

"I don't feel so good," she answered.

"Take the afternoon off," said Nelson. "This weather's getting to everyone. It's quiet anyway." She stooped to pick up the plates, but Nelson stopped her and motioned for her to leave. Corazón mechanically removed her apron and got her purse out of the closet. She didn't remember walking home.

Corazón skipped supper that evening. She went to bed early, saying that her head hurt.

"Well, what's wrong with *her?*" said Queenie sarcastically. She was on her way to meet Art, and pouted her lips in the hall mirror to make sure her lipstick was right.

That night, Corazón's bed was rocked by steep waves. She hung on desperately and gulped ragged breaths of air as each wave rose up and up before crashing down on her. The room tipped from side to side and the wind screamed as Corazón clung to the blankets and shut her eyes tightly.

Finally, Corazón could hold on no more and was wrenched from the bed and thrown into the depths of the black sea. Her lungs burning, she gasped and her mouth filled with water. A searing pain tore her in two before she gasped one last time and her lungs burst.

The stormy sea quieted. Corazón drifted up, lifted on a stream of bubbles. She pitied the poor creature lying on the sea bottom, pale and spent, its hair in its eyes. She brushed back her own luxuriant green tendrils before darting off to join her sisters.

◊ ◊ ◊

They found Corazón the next morning lying on the floor, limp as a wrung-out washrag. A line of salt crusted her upper lip, and there was sand under her nails. A stroke, said the doctor, brought on by the heat and dehydration.

When her clenched fist was pried open, a rough, pink object fell out. Coral, shaped like a heart.

"That's Art's," said Queenie, and was suddenly silent.

Art had sailed that morning for Japan, and wasn't due to return for a long time.

Corazón opened her eyes just then and looked at her sister, unable to speak. Queenie, crying, left the room.

Corazón stayed in the hospital for several days, then home for many weeks, propped in a chair by the window. When her sister delivered a baby the following spring, Corazón moved into an apartment with her to help take care of the little girl. Jade, as they called her, had eyes the color of seawater, or of a Texas sky just before a storm.

Corazón gradually got well, but everyone agreed that she was different after that. She moved with a purposeful stride, and wheeled her sister's baby down the street like they were on parade. Sometimes she disappeared for days at a time, and people said that she was meeting a man in Galveston. Others said that she returned with the strong smell of seaweed on her and a wild look in her copper eyes. But everyone agreed that she wore a pink stone at her throat, suspended on a thin gold chain, and shaped exactly like a human heart.

GYPSY LOVER

Every woman should have a gypsy lover on the side. At least that's what my sister said, with such conviction that I was inclined to believe her—my sister, who'd never even had a boyfriend.

When we were really little, our mother used to try to make us stay with her in a crowd by saying that if we wandered away, the gypsies would steal us. This made me hope that they would, and I had very specific ideas about the sort of gypsies I hoped would steal me. They would live in covered wagons drawn by big, gentle horses with heavy bells on their harnesses, and we would build a campfire every night.

I don't know that I ever discussed this with my sister, but we both seemed to have the same ideas about gypsies. It was quite a few years later when my sister made this statement, when she was in her early teens and I was about eleven.

"Every woman should have a gypsy lover on the side," she said, standing and looking at herself in the mirror, turning her head this way and that. She stood kind of sideways, trying to stick her hip out, I think, but she had no hips.

I remember that I was shocked to hear her use words like "woman" and "lover." It made her seem sophisticated and worldly, although she wasn't at all. My sister read Emily Dickinson and played the violin in the school orchestra. Maybe it was the violin that made her say that. Gypsies were supposed to play violins in the circle of light around a campfire while people threw heavy gold coins at their feet.

My sister was wearing a flowered shift when she said this, turning her head and looking at herself in an appraising way. The shift didn't look that great on her, the colors were wrong; I wanted her to give it to me. It was a hot September afternoon, maybe as hot as it got all summer. The room was stifling, and my sister looked pale in the heat, with large, tragic dark eyes, Anne Frank eyes —maybe the kind of eyes that would charm a gypsy.

"Why?" I said. "Why not marry a gypsy?"

She shook her head no, but otherwise didn't answer me. I would remember all this later, quite awhile after the night she didn't come home. Otherwise I don't think I would have remembered that day at all.

Once, the kids at the bus stop said some gypsies had moved onto their block. My neighbor Sylvia Gonzalez and I had to get up at five a.m. and walk seven blocks to catch our bus in a rough, all-white neighborhood. Sylvia was a year older and prepared to defend me to the death, since I was skinny and wore glasses and was generally assumed to be incapable of taking care of myself. This saved me from any serious fights all the way through high school in a city where people were commonly knifed or shot in school parking lots. Our bus driver, a black woman, kept a heavy pipe under her seat and was terrified of all of us—black, white, and brown alike. This gave us a sense of power and self-importance which evaporated as soon as we got to school, where city police stood at the high gates and on the rooftops watching us, nightsticks and cans of Mace at the ready.

I remember a boy, small for his age, who was supposed to be from the gypsy family. He had dark red hair and freckles, a first name that seemed to be short for something, and an Italian last name. He was quiet. The other kids teased him about his name being a girl's name—something like Sal—but they mostly left him alone. There was something about him that made me think he really might be a gypsy—his aloneness, as of someone who has had to move a lot, or some invisible mark about him, like the glint of an amulet under his shirt. He rode the bus irregularly for about three or four weeks, then he was gone.

That's how it was with my sister. One day she was just gone. She had walked to the library with some friends, and my mother was supposed to pick her up at 8:30, but she wasn't there. My mother came home, thinking she had gotten a ride with someone else, but as it got later and later, the evening turned into a night of loud conversations, of the phone ringing, and driving back to the library and around the neighborhood, and finally the awful calling the police.

We could all feel that something was wrong. A policeman came over and talked to my parents, then went out and looked for her. I don't remember everything that happened, just thinking that a police car, common in our neighborhood, was parked in front of *our* house, which meant that something bad had happened to us.

We found out that my sister had been offered a ride home with someone else's mother, but she had decided to wait for ours. It had been exactly 8:30, and she figured my mother had already left the house, so it was too late to call and say she had a ride.

I can almost see her standing on the wet lawn of the library in the twilight, the sun just gone down in the spectacular red and orange sunsets we got from the smog. She was wearing red slacks and a white blouse with little pleats on the front, and a baggy brown sweater. She always carried lots of books and a little square purse. Her long black hair was held back from her face with white barrettes. No one ever saw her again.

A thousand times I've imagined the gypsy cart as it turned the corner and rumbled slowly down the street, pulling to a slow stop in front of the library. How my sister stepped up to pet the snorting horses, and couldn't resist when the man on the seat offered her a ride. He would have had long black hair pulled back in a pony tail, green eyes, and one earring. He would have been wearing scuffed black boots and baggy pants and a full white shirt under a black velvet vest. A woman would lean out of the covered part of the wagon, which was lit from inside by a kerosene lamp, and smile at my sister.

"It's all right," she would have said. "We'll give you a ride just to the corner."

And my sister would have handed up her books and climbed onto the hard wooden seat, and maybe the driver let her hold the reins. That's how I imagined it happened.

By the end of the next day my parents were angry. They hadn't slept all night. My father went to work but came home early to drive around and look for her. My parents were angry because the police had suggested she might be a runaway. The police weren't taking it seriously. My parents were angry at my sister for disappearing, and probably would have killed her if she had come home that day or the next. Ours was not a happy home, but it was not one you would run away from. It would have been too much trouble if you were caught.

Besides, my sister had no reason to run away that I knew of. My parents kept asking me questions about her. What she said. What her friends were like. If she'd ever talked about running away. It made me realize that I didn't know very much about my sister. She was in high school and I was in junior high, so I didn't know her friends any better than my parents did. She was good and smart and all her friends were good and smart and came from families who lived in better neighborhoods— neighborhoods where Mexicans couldn't live.

I think my parents felt humiliated. They were worried, but they seemed to be as worried about what everybody thought as they were about my sister. They were from poor families, and had worked hard to establish themselves as decent, middle-class people. They had a lot of ideas about how decent people looked and acted, and they didn't include having your fifteen-year-old daughter disappear. Even if she had come back, her reputation would have been ruined. These were things my parents felt they understood. They did not understand the silence, the unspoken accusation that they had done something wrong to bring about my sister's disappearance. My mother cried constantly and her eyes were rimmed in bright red. She looked terrible.

During this time I remembered something that my sister had done when I was very little. She had entered a speech contest where she recited a poem about Scottish children who die while saving their kinsmen, by taking a message across a freezing stream. That was the first time I'd heard the word "kin." My mother and aunt, conferring with each other in Spanish, had coached her on their idea of a Scottish accent.

"The water is *cald*," I remember her saying over and over until they were satisfied. "The water is *cald*."

When she had learned it from beginning to end, they made her stand on a chair in the kitchen, where she recited, or more precisely, acted out the story of the poem with great feeling. I was so moved by the tragic fate of the innocent children that I cried. It wasn't until weeks after her disappearance that I remembered the remark about gypsies and figured out what happened to her.

They would have come around the corner from Eighth Street, the clomp-clomping of the horses and their bells audible for some time before she would have seen them. It was just getting really dark as the last light faded from the western sky, and the lamp inside would have made the canvas of the wagon glow a warm yellow. The man driving would have talked and whistled softly to the horses, which wore blinders. They would have pulled slowly to a stop in front of the library, giving my sister plenty of time to run away if she had wanted to. She would have stood transfixed by the sight, the lantern light shining on her pale face and big, dark eyes. And the gypsy couple would have seen that she was just the person for their son to marry when he grew up. They went slowly up the street, my sister on the buckboard seat, turning the corner just as my mother pulled up. She could have heard the horses' hooves and the bells jingling if she had only listened.

They would have continued north, up the quiet streets of houses lit only by the feeble glow of televisions, past the high school, past my junior high school, up past Highland Street and Sepulveda and Waterman, up to the foothills where their gypsy camp waited in a grove of eucalyptus trees. They would have camped on the old Coolie Ranch, a piece of property vacant and for sale for nearly thirty years. There would have been a big bonfire, and the woman would have put a warm black shawl around my sister's shoulders, and she would have seen her future husband for the first time—also fifteen, tall and skinny, with green eyes like his father. That's what would make her stay, that and the horses, which she would get up and feed early every morning, sometimes braiding flowers into their manes.

◇ ◇ ◇

Our family was never the same after that. My father went to work and came home and watched television until it was time for bed. We ate dinner in front of the television, only speaking when necessary. Even though I was lonelier than ever, I joined clubs to get out of the house. My mother made me tell her exactly when I would get home, exactly how long it would take to do anything, until we were all obsessed with time. She never said, though, that the gypsies might steal me. I don't know if she remembered having ever said that to us at all.

I thought my sister might write to us, or at least to me. I imagined postcards from the Midwest, written with a cheap pen by the light of a fire, smelling of wood smoke. I imagined that they taught her how to juggle and how she and the boy, later her husband, would juggle flaming sticks that they tossed higher and higher in the air as people oohed and aahed. The boy wore a square-cornered hat which he doffed at the end and collected money in, always heavy gold coins, though I don't know where people got gold coins like that in this country.

I imagined that my sister, always a good writer, kept a diary about the life that she lived, and had kept an accounting of every day since the night she went away. She would keep it under her bunk in the wagon, in a secret drawer with her jewelry. My sister would have looked a born gypsy if dressed for the part. No one would have guessed where she came from.

I imagined that they went to different parts of the country depending on the season, and that they had many relatives who also lived in gypsy bands. Some of them were with circuses and lived in Europe part of the year. I watched Don Ameche's television show about the great circuses of Europe, searching the faces carefully for anyone who looked like my sister. Some of the gypsy families probably sang. My sister could have sung and played the tambourine. She could drop her shyness the way she dropped it to recite a speech or a poem, then step back into it like a cloak.

◊ ◊ ◊

Sometimes after work, when it's too hot to go right home and there's nothing else to do, I drive slowly north from our part of the city, past Highland Street, Sepulveda and Waterman, up to where the new subdivisions start. I park on Rinconada, or Rodeo or Camellia, somewhere near where the old Coolie Ranch sign used to be, where the eucalyptus grove used to sigh and whisper in the wind. People out here aren't used to seeing a car as old as mine, so I have to park in different places to avoid suspicion. I watch the sun dull into gold and pink, sinking slowly into the Santa Fe railroad yards, although you can't see them from here. But I've known since I was a child that the sun always sets in the Santa Fe yards, and I've lived my life to the rhythms of its trains coming and going, coming and going—the whistle at noon, and the whistle at midnight.

I rest my chin on the steering wheel and picture the gypsy camp. I imagine that they sing and play music until very late around an open campfire; the children, dozing in the wagons, fight sleep to hear one last story or song. Then the adults drink wine or smoke hashish and fall into a sort of trance, perhaps sharing ancestral memories. My sister's ancestral memories would probably be pretty bloodthirsty, since we're Mexican and our ancestors practiced human sacrifice, so maybe she doesn't smoke the hashish. Maybe she just drinks red wine or thick Turkish coffee with lots of sugar.

When I think of my sister, she's lying back on a tasseled pillow in a gypsy wagon, not much older than she was ten years ago, watching people smoke a water pipe while she drinks from a brass cup. Her eyes are rimmed with kohl (aren't every gypsy's eyes?) and her lips are relaxed and reddened from the drink. No one around her knows that she once stood on a chair and recited a poem about brave Scottish children, and no one knows that she once played the violin as wildly and sweetly as any gypsy lover in her mind.

REFLECTION IN THE EYE OF A CROW

W e sat in the bedroom surrounded by white sheets and pillowcases. I embroidered while my sister read. The window exploded in a thousand glass shards which glistened against the white linen. A crow lay stunned in the middle of the floor. My sister ran screaming from the room.

The curtains billowed in from the broken window, and I could smell the ocean a thousand miles away. As my sister ran shrieking through the house, the crow raised its head and looked at me as if about to speak.

◇ ◇ ◇

Sometimes I'm afraid I'll wake and be like Prudencia—the glittering stare, sallow skin, hair like dried leaves hanging from a tree. I can hear the crow harshness of her voice, and feel that edge in my throat on certain mornings.

There is madness in the family—the terror of a quiet afternoon, the unbearable emptiness of an open doorway. How can I fight her insistence that I am weak, I don't feel well, there must be something wrong?

"Hear my prayer, O Lord!" I read. "I resemble a pelican in the wilderness; I have become like an owl in the waste places. I lie awake, and have become like a lonely bird on a housetop." I walk through the Valley of the Shadow, and the shadow weighs upon me like a wing-shaped burden; others see it in my eyes, and shun me.

◇ ◇ ◇

I remember a villa with sparkling fountains behind locked iron gates. It is in a city with a strange name. It is far from the sea, and very old. No one is left to embroider my handkerchiefs or shop for vegetables in the public market. No one is left but cripples and insomniacs and a painter who cannot bear the sight of the human body.

The maid came to change the unclean sheets, but a knife was found concealed in her skirts. I locked the door just as the handle turned. She was let go, but I still hear her footsteps in the courtyard.

I will stay indoors and wash my hair. It is better to burn in secret than admit unhappiness. I will hide between the pages of a book, the gospel according to Prudencia, which has no Song of Solomon.

Every Good Friday, the hymnals bled during the evening service. They always blamed me. Prudencia would pull the velvet ribbon tighter around my neck, and my tears would fall upon the pages. The thin paper would wrinkle like the skin of an old woman as we sang, "Nearer My God To Thee."

I see her in my child, the one I was not fit to bear— the vacant look, the fear of empty rooms and billowing curtains. I see the hair spring away from her face, the mouth set like stitches in a row. There is madness in her mirror, pain in her breast from where a plate was shoved in the darkened dining room.

◇ ◇ ◇

I will study my lessons; God told her just what to say: Thou shalt not think. Thou shalt not be free. Thou shalt not seek happiness in this land of strangers, for their ways are not ours. Thou shalt not cry out, for mine is the Power.

I cannot bear the lingering touch of a woman's hand. I am forever chaste, forever violated in that web of hair and words and unspoken threats. The magenta hair ribbon is wound twice, and again around my neck, and I feel the tears like falling birds upon my face. Those who see the ribbon turn away. It is not our business, they say. It is a family matter. My hands bleed like stigmata, and I place my Bible over the stains on my white dress.

The wood creaks as I walk across the veranda. It feels cool beneath my sandals. A man is waiting inside. I do not know his name, but his eyes called to me in the plaza. I try to open the heavy wooden door, but cannot. I can just fit the tips of my fingers in the bulletholes that scar its surface. The air is heavy with the smell of jacaranda and oranges.

I wear orthopedic stockings and sit in a darkened room, moaning softly to myself. The hair ribbon is cut short and placed as a marker in my Bible. Shawls cover the furniture, and people speak softly outside the heavy door. No one speaks to me. I must study my lessons: Humility. Obedience. Servitude. To be dead in Christ. I want to laugh, a harsh sound that threatens to break free and fly around the room beating its wings against the windows, but I swallow it back and say nothing.

◇ ◇ ◇

I cannot laugh or dance, or throw rose petals over the sea when the moon is full. The aurora borealis pierces the edge of my city, a call to remembrance. I must sit in a quiet room and embroider pages with my words: Desire. Flowering Quince. Cocoon.

I see my pain reflected in my husband's eyes. He is afraid of me, afraid of who I am, and of what I might become: the wounded deer, the weeping madonna, the witch with the crow in her throat.

The curtains billow in and wrap me in a white shroud. I cannot cry or move until the bird lifts its head as if about to speak. I raise the dagger concealed in my skirt and look away.

MRS. VARGAS AND THE DEAD NATURALIST

Mrs. Vargas had been cleaning the house for a week in anticipation of the visit, and the guest wasn't due for at least three more days. The hemp floormats had been beaten and aired out, the white-washed walls scrubbed inside and out, and Mrs. Vargas was now spreading her best embroidered tablecloth on the big square table in the sala while admonishing her family not to spill anything on it for the next few days. When she heard the thump on the door, she thought it was a neighbor.

"¡Entren!" she said loudly. Mrs. Vargas, a short, sturdy woman, fluttered her hands over her hair as she started towards the door. The handle turned, and a dusty figure half-walked, half-fell into the front room. She had never seen him before.

"Dr. Ellis?" she said, "Dr. Ellis?" Receiving no answer, she helped him to a wicker chair. The Anglo was green-ish-white, and a cold sweat stood on his forehead and upper lip. Panting heavily, he said nothing, but looked up at her with pleading eyes.

"¡Agua!" she yelled. "Just a minute, I'll bring you some water." And she patted him into the chair as though that would keep him from falling over while she went for cold water. Returning from the kitchen with her daughter, she could see that it was too late. He was slumped over and not breathing.

Nevertheless, she said, "Luz, go get the curandera, and you," she said to her other children, attracted by the commotion, "help me put him on the bed." A leather folder fell to the floor as they carried the dusty man to the guest bedroom and laid his body on the clean cotton bedspread.

As she had suspected, the naturalist was quite dead by the time help arrived.

"It was his heart," said the curandera. "Besides, he drank too much. That's why he's so yellow."

The man looked older than Mrs. Vargas had imagined, and was not well dressed. He wore a torn black raincoat completely unsuited to the Yucatec climate, a cheap cotton shirt, and polyester pants that were frayed at the cuffs. He wasn't at all what she had expected.

"Dear Claudia," the letter from her sister in Mérida had begun. "I have a favor to ask of you. A man my husband sometimes works for, a famous naturalist, would like to go to our village to study the *ikeek*, which the Americans call the rockbird. Since there is no place to stay, I thought you might be able to accommodate him for a few days. I am sure that he would be very appreciative of the favor. Please let me know if this will be all right." Mrs. Vargas had quickly written back, mindful of the prestige which might result from having a famous naturalist as her guest in the village.

As the curandera was finishing up, the priest arrived.

"What happened?" he asked.

"He had a heart attack and died," said Mrs. Vargas. "I guess the journey was too much for him."

"Is it the scientist?" he asked.

"Well, he's an American. Who else would it be?" Then Mrs. Vargas remembered the portfolio. Finding it on the floor, she and the priest unzipped its stiff edges and looked inside. It contained colored pencils and drawings of tropical birds on very thin paper.

"But how did he get here?" asked the priest. "The bus doesn't come this far. And where is his luggage? His passport?"

No one knew the answers to these questions. By now, a crowd had gathered outside.

"We saw him walking up the road," said Saladino Chan, "as we were returning from the fields. He asked the way to Mrs. Vargas' house. He didn't have any luggage then, and he didn't look well."

"Maybe he walked from Napual, where the bus stops, and forgot his suitcase. Or maybe he was robbed." Yes, nodded everyone, or maybe he was having it sent later, with special scientific equipment. In any case, it would be of no help to him now.

Mrs. Vargas perched on a chair for a minute to collect her thoughts. She was upset by the death, but at the same time, the prone figure in the bedroom filled her with uneasiness. She wasn't sure just what sort of a guest he would have been, anyway.

After administering the last rites to Dr. Ellis, the priest returned to the front room and sat down opposite Mrs. Vargas. "We could take the body by truck to Napuatl, and put it on the bus back to Mérida," said the priest, "but it is very hot, and I'm afraid the body will deteriorate. I think we should bury him here."

"Yes—" said Mrs. Vargas, perking up a little, "at least we can give him a nice funeral."

So a black wooden coffin was prepared for the naturalist, and the stonemason carved his name on a slab of marble he'd been saving for something special. The next morning, the coffin was covered with the bright flowers of the hyacinth, and the blossoms of the silkcotton tree. The coffin bearers sang the songs for the dead as they marched in procession to the cemetery, and the whole village turned out for the occasion.

"God respects those who respect his creations, and scientists who study birds and flowers, in their own way, respect and conserve God's work," said the priest. The people nodded, final prayers were said, and the coffin was lowered into the rocky grave. Everyone gave their condolences to Mrs. Vargas, since the naturalist had no family present.

After that, the men went off to the fields, and everyone agreed that it was the best funeral they'd had in a while. The bill for the headstone would be sent to the university.

Mrs. Vargas, still crying a little, hurried home to write to her sister and tell her the bad news. The cotton bedspread was washed, and her three younger boys, who had been sent to stay with cousins, moved back into the guest bedroom.

Three days later, a Toyota Land Cruiser roared into the village. An American asked directions to Mrs. Vargas' house, and drove on.

"It must be someone from the American consulate," said the villagers, finding an excuse to walk up the road that led to Mrs. Vargas' house.

The Land Cruiser stopped in front, and out jumped a trim, athletic man in his mid-thirties. He was not dressed like a diplomat, but instead wore a khaki shirt and trousers.

"Mrs. Vargas?" he asked, when she opened the door. "I'm Dr. Ellis, from the university," and he smiled his best American smile.

An expression between horror and ecstasy crossed her face and, with a little cry, Mrs. Vargas swooned into her daughter's arms. Luz, confused and scared, burst into tears while the naturalist stood in the doorway, unsure whether to try and help, shifting the strap to his expensive camera uncomfortably on his shoulder.

Finally, Mrs. Vargas blinked her eyes and, assuring the man that she was all right, offered him a chair and described the death of a few days before.

"What did he look like?" asked Dr. Ellis.

"An older man with yellow skin," she said, "and a black raincoat. He carried a leather envelope with pictures of birds."

"How strange," said Ellis. "I have no idea who that could have been. Didn't he have a passport or anything?"

"No," said Mrs. Vargas. "We found nothing in his pockets, and he had no luggage. All he brought were the drawings."

At her mother's bidding, Luz brought out the worn portfolio, and Ellis opened it. He carefully examined the drawings, which were unsigned, and turned the folder inside out looking for clues, but there was nothing. The colored pencils had been manufactured in Mexico, and were the sort commonly used by schoolchildren.

"I don't know what to tell you," said Ellis, "except that people sometimes write to the university, or call, if they think they've seen something unusual. He might have called after I left and found out I'd be here. But I don't know anything about him. I'm sorry."

Mrs. Vargas recalled the acrid smell of the dead man's skin, and her sense of foreboding returned. "I thought there was something odd about him. He didn't look right."

"I'm very sorry about the mixup," said Dr. Ellis. "If I can compensate you, or someone, for the burial expenses, I would like to do that. I guess someone should notify the authorities, if it hasn't been done. I would be happy to take care of it."

He waited for a response from Mrs. Vargas, who sat with her hands folded in her lap. She seemed to have forgotten him.

"Oh, yes," she said finally. "I'm sure it can be worked out." She realized that the young scientist was waiting to be invited to remain. "If the circumstances permit, I hope that you will stay and continue with your work."

"If that's all right," he answered. "After all the confusion, I hope it's not too much trouble."

"Not at all," she answered. "My house is your house."

So the three younger boys went out the back door to their cousins' again, while Dr. Ellis brought his suitcase and several six-packs of Orange Crush in the front door. He opened and gave a bottle to each of the remaining children, and they drank the warm soda right before dinner, much to Mrs. Vargas' consternation, but she said nothing.

At dinner, on the old tablecloth, since the good one had been soiled in the meantime, Dr. Ellis gave her a fancy silver salt and pepper set.

"I thought you might like these," he said. She thanked him profusely and placed them out on the table. She didn't tell him that she would never use them, since the high humidity made salt stick together and it would clog up the little holes in the shaker.

Dr. Ellis told them about his work. He taught ornithology at the university, and studied the birds of southern Mexico and Guatemala. The rockbird was of interest because it is one of the few species of birds that maintains a *lek,* or dancing ground, which the male clears on the jungle floor in order to display his beautiful feathers and attract a mate.

"The reported sightings near your village," continued Dr. Ellis, "if confirmed, would make this the farthest north this type of bird has ever been found in the Americas. It would change the maps of ornithology!" The family nodded politely and ate their beans and tortillas. They didn't tell him that he would sleep that night where the dead man had lain.

The next morning, Dr. Ellis set out early to find the rockbird. Overtaking some farmers on the way to their fields, he asked if they had seen the small, yellow bird.

"Oh, yes," they said nervously, "it has been seen. Out there. It lives out in the jungle." But no one seemed to know just where.

Late that afternoon, on his way back to the village, Ellis stopped by the cemetery to pay his respects, and saw the tombstone with his own name on it. He went into town to the cantina, found the stonemason, and offered to pay for the tombstone, if he would just take it down. After a few beers, and after having ascertained that the real occupant of the grave was penniless and unknown, the mason decided to reuse the stone on another occasion, and would put up a wooden cross instead. He was very grateful for the handsome pen and pencil set which the scientist gave to him.

Ellis noticed that, as he walked down the street, people shrank back to let him pass, and were careful not to let even their clothing touch him. Whispers followed him, and a few of the older women even crossed themselves. The next morning, walking out to the jungle with the farmers, he saw that the headstone with his name on it had been taken down, and additional, plain stones had been piled onto the already mounded grave.

"Why are there more stones on the grave?" he asked.

"Just to make sure," was the answer.

Again, he searched fruitlessly for any sign of the rockbird. The drawings in the portfolio had included one of a yellow bird, but it looked more like a glorified canary than anything else. Ellis suspected that it had been traced from another picture. Again that evening, he asked the villagers if they had ever seen the bird, and instead of specific answers, received only vague, affirmative answers.

Finally, the curandera said to him, "We only see the *ikeek,* as we call it, when someone in the village is about to die. The bird waits to accompany the spirit back to the gates of heaven, so that it won't get lost."

After that, Ellis stopped asking the villagers for help, but continued to search the jungles on his own for two more days. He found a single yellow feather that could have belonged to any bird at all, but he took a picture of it, wrote down the location, and sealed it up in a little plastic envelope for further analysis.

Disappointed by his lack of findings, and put off by the villagers' superstitions, Dr. Ellis decided to return to Mérida. Mrs. Vargas was relieved to see him go, but cried in spite of herself. The children walked along behind the Land Cruiser as he slowly made his way back through the village towards the main road.

As Dr. Ellis headed for the highway north, the villagers wondered if his visit would bring them bad luck; the priest wondered if God had taken care of the dead man's soul, although all of the prayers had been said in Dr. Ellis' name; and Mrs. Vargas decided that her sister in Mérida owed her a big favor.

In the jungle, under the tangle of vines and fallen trees, the rockbird stomped and shook out its golden feathers on its carefully groomed square yard of bare ground, little knowing that it was the cause of so much trouble.

The mystery of the dead American was never solved. The mayor received a letter from the American consulate, saying that a representative would be sent to investigate, but no one ever came. Two or three people claimed to have seen the old man standing outside of the village at dusk in his tattered raincoat. It was an evil spirit all along, said some, come to stir up trouble in the village. If the coffin were to be opened, nothing would be found inside but cornhusks. But Mrs. Vargas never doubted the reality of the man she had helped prepare for burial.

◇ ◇ ◇

The night that Mrs. Vargas awoke with moonlight on the foot of the bed and heard a noise outside, she knew that the dead man had returned. A wind blew from the east, whistling around the edges of the house. A lonely dog was barking. Mrs. Vargas got up and walked barefoot into the front room in her long, cotton night-gown, her black and silver braids down her back. She knew what she had to do. Feeling for the worn leather portfolio which had taken up residence under the sofa, Mrs. Vargas then unlatched the front door.

Even in the moonlight, his complexion looked un-healthy, his coat dusty and torn. The wind made wisps of hair stand up on his head, then lie down again.

Not daring to speak, Mrs. Vargas threw the portfolio as far as she could away from the house, across the road into the waiting jungle. The man bowed slightly, a wistful look on his face, and turned away. Mrs. Vargas slammed the door, locked it, and returned to her bedroom. And all the living, and all the dead were in place.

THE FIRE OF SAN MARCOS

T he decrepit old woman who lived at the edge of town had predicted a storm for the Festival of San Marcos, but the children just laughed at her dramatic statements.

"Rain and fire will fall from the sky," she screeched, shaking her bony finger at the white-hot expanse that pressed down upon the sleepy town. Not a cloud was to be seen.

"Go buy yourself some new clothes," the children yelled at the scarecrow figure. "Buy yourself a new hat for the Festival."

"A black day!" she screeched after them. "A black day!"

On the other side of town, Marcos Romeros stood outside smoking, a skeptical eye turned towards the sky. He needed good weather for that evening, for he was a pirotécnico, a fireworks specialist brought in for the occasion.

It was late summer in Los Picos, and the air was thick with humidity and anticipation. It was the Day of San Marcos, the town's patron saint. Every lamppost was hung with a garland, and every statue had a wreath of yellow flowers at its base. The shopkeepers had chased off the dogs and swept the sidewalks in front of their doorways.

Their houses stood in freshly whitewashed splendor on the green and brown hillside.

In honor of the occasion, the local theater troupe was staging a presentation of a play by Sophocles. Juan Suárez de Mejía, general manager of the theater and director of the acting group, had shortened and rewritten the play for local tastes and renamed it *Las Nubes—The Clouds*.

"Come, ye swift and vengeful Furies, glut your wrath on all the host, and spare not!" yelled Ajax. As if on cue, thunder rumbled ominously off the nearby hills. Rain began to pelt the tin roofs of the houses, and soon water was pouring through several holes in the theater roof, where neighbors had borrowed material for their own badly leaking homes. The audience remained dry, since the slope of the roof funneled the water onto the stage. The actors gamely continued the play, skirting the puddles that were beginning to form around them.

"...And so with thee and thy fierce speech—perchance a great tempest, though its breath come from a little cloud, shall quench thy blustering," intoned Menelaus. With that, lightning struck nearby, and the theater was plunged into complete, watery darkness. While the audience wondered if this was a special effect, Teucer called out his lines from one spot, not daring to move about on the invisible stage.

As it became clear that the power outage was more than temporary, Suárez made his way out onto the black stage, slipping and falling once in the puddles.

"I'm sorry, ladies and gentlemen," he said, "but we are unable to continue our drama without light. Thank you for your forbearance. You are all invited back tomorrow night, at no charge, to see the complete performance. Please bring your ticket stubs from tonight. Thank you."

By now, all the ranchers and tourists were wide awake, and slightly confused by the series of events. Almost wordlessly, they filed out of the auditorium into the relative brilliance of the zócalo, the main plaza, where a clear, peaceful night showed no signs of the thunderstorm. As abruptly as it had arrived, the violent electrical disturbance had moved off over the mountains. Power had been restored, and the zócalo, smelling of new-washed stone, glowed pristinely under the streetlamps.

Marcos Romeros, known in some parts of Mexico as the most brilliant pirotécnico in the world, worked feverishly in a nearby warehouse to make sure that the display would be ready on time. The play having ended early, town officials were pressuring him to go on as soon as possible, so as not to lose the crowds. A man of minimal speech, he worked in silence with his five sons as they tamped and tied and crimped in final preparation for the show in honor of San Marcos. It was a flattery to his holy spirit, and a plea for a good harvest in the following months. Everything had to be perfect. Marcos Romeros would not have it any other way.

Dozens of young women primped before going onstage in the plaza, where a beauty pageant would be held. The brief downpour had ruined some of their hairdos. They wore high heels, straight skirts, and glamorous amounts of makeup. Girls who had looked sixteen that morning now took on the airs of seasoned movie stars. Some of them smoked or stamped their feet impatiently as the waiting went on and on.

The mayor, perspiration running down his cheeks and into his white collar, finally stepped onto a raised plat-form at one end of the plaza and yelled something unin-telligible into the microphone. Feedback and dissonance accompanied the mayor's hoarse speech.

The girls lined up and paraded across the platform. The contest took place rather quickly, considering the delay which had preceded it. Speeches were made, girls' names were called, they cried, and roses and sashes were handed out—La reina de la fiesta, la reina de la mies, las princesas de quien sabe qué—everyone was made either a queen or a princess. They stood shoulder to shoulder, beaming and throwing kisses. The platform sagged under the weight of so much beauty.

With the pageant finished, the plaza filled with chil-dren and families anticipating the fireworks, and a few eager boys exploded their own firecrackers as they waited. A show by Marcos Romeros was very special. The town officials had vied with several other towns to have him perform that night, and he would move on with his wife and sons to the village of Ojuelos the next day, on his way eventually to Guanajuato, there to celebrate the Day of the Dead, as his father and grandfather had be-fore him. The dead were preserved in the earth of Guanajuato, and were especially in need of a good fire-works display to soothe their restless souls.

But for now, the celebration was for the living. After another garbled speech by the mayor, colored sprays of light shot up around the speakers' platform, waterfalls flowing backwards into the sky. This was followed by fireworks that turned cartwheels just below roof level. These were hard to see from the back of the crowd, and people pressed closer and closer. Tiny children balanced on their parents' shoulders, yelling little exclamation points of joy into the night air.

After that, all eyes turned to a twenty-foot pole which had been erected, like a mast, to the right of the stage. Poles had been lashed across it, and various mysterious objects were fastened to it, with a white disk at the very top. Marcos, dressed in peasant whites, stepped up to the pole and, with his cigarette, lit the fuse at the base.

A lone cry rose from the back of the crowd, and people turned in time to see an old woman running off into the darkness.

"La loca," they said, pointing at their heads. "The fireworks have upset her."

White sparks flew in every direction as the lowest display caught fire. The few dignitaries remaining on the platform quickly jumped off, and the crowd drew back to leave a wide, clear space around the pole. Into this arena pranced little boys holding newspapers over their heads, leaping and dancing barefoot in the shower of sparks. Marcos stood, unconcerned for his own safety, against the building directly behind the pole, stepping out once to relight the fuse when it sputtered between displays.

Each display was more astounding than the last. Roman candles and Piccolo Petes, spinners and gaudy explosions that threatened to engulf the whole sky, then fizzled to mere whispers upon the still night air. The crowd was mesmerized with both fright and awe, red and green and blue reflecting in their upturned faces. Marcos

Romeros stood with the sparks falling all around him, a peaceful smile of satisfaction on his face.

As the fuse worked its way closer to the top, each display scattered sparks over a wider and wider area of the crowd until they could no longer be avoided, and the people finally stood resigned to the fire of San Marcos, shading their eyes to see the brilliance all around them.

Before taking light, the white disk hesitated, then sprouted two jets of blue flame. It began to spin around and around, and to emit a high, whistling noise. Faster and faster, and louder and louder it got, until the disk reached such a point of frenzy that it flung itself scream-ing from the pole and sailed off into the night like a wild banshee, or a flying saucer returning home.

The ensuing silence settled like a satisfied sigh over the crowd. The plaza began to empty as people made their way home, carrying sleepy children, or to the church for a midnight mass, the last act of the Festival of San Marcos.

Much later that night, many people heard sirens in their sleep, but there are often sirens in Los Picos. It is a sign of civilization. The next morning, however, the newspaper carried some terrible news: *EXPLOSIÓN HORRIBLE—Cuatro muertos*. The warehouse where the fireworks were assembled had caught fire early that morn-ing, and Marcos Romeros and two of his sons, after hav-ing dashed inside to save the inventory meant for Ojuelos, had been killed by a huge explosion. A fireman was killed later when the roof collapsed. Another lightning storm during the early morning hours was suspected as the cause of the fire.

People stood in quiet groups on the street corners, shivering in the early morning air. Details of the catastrophe were muttered under the brims of straw Stetsons and whispered behind fringed shawls. The explosion had been so violent, and the heat of the fire so intense, that no trace had been found of Marcos Romeros or his two sons. The flames had consumed them completely.

Juan Suárez de Mejía, sipping his morning coffee while he read the news, couldn't help but think that the play had, in fact, been given a fitting end. Ajax was to be punished by the gods for reaching too far above his station, but the storm and power outage had cut the drama short. The fireworks display, however, had been worthy of a god; it had been too perfect, and Marcos Romeros had paid dearly.

The warehouse stood gutted and open only a half-block from the plaza, and red plastic ribbon had been put up to keep the curious at a safe distance. The same little boys who had danced in the sparks the night before now stared at the widow in her long black dress as she searched through the ruins. At times, she stopped and uttered an unearthly wail of sorrow.

Almost bent double with the pain of her grieving heart, the widow Romeros sifted through the ashes for some sign of her husband and two sons. A gleaming object caught her eye. She rummaged through the wet ashes, throwing away chunks of black debris, until she got her hand on it and brought it up to the light. She stared at it. There in the palm of her hand were her husband's false teeth. He had bought them from an American dentist in Ciudad Juárez and had been very proud of them. The teeth were not even scorched, although nothing else remained.

People gasped and pointed as she held them up, each tooth gleaming in the early morning light. A ragged old woman who had been standing at the edge of the crowd sighed, crossed herself, and slowly walked away.

The widow took the teeth, wrapped in a handkerchief, to the church to have them blessed.

"Ah!" said Father Arzuba, closely examining the dentures. "This is a mystery indeed! I think you should leave them here, for, God willing, the preservation of these teeth may be a miracle."

The widow was unsure.

"I don't know," she said. "This is all I have left of him in this world, besides my three sons, the Virgin preserve them. He was a great man, and I'm not sure that this is the right thing to do."

"I will write up a description of the event," said Father Arzuba, "and send it to the archbishop. But these things take time, and I will need proof of the miracle. Aside from witnesses, this is the only proof. Besides," he added, a sudden inspiration, "I will keep them at the feet of San Marcos in the church, our protector against lightning and hail; and since your husband, too, was named Marcos, God rest his soul, every celebration of the Festival of San Marcos will also be in memory of Marcos Romeros. People will always think of him."

The widow finally agreed, but only on the condition that her sons be allowed to present the fireworks display every year on this occasion.

A few shovelfuls of ash were buried in three coffins as the remains of Marcos Romeros and his two sons. After the funeral, the rest of the family moved on to purchase new supplies and start over again.

The wreaths and garlands were taken down, and the town council began a never-ending argument on how to safely store fireworks. Some wanted a concrete bunker, such as those used by the highway crews for storing dynamite, but that would be expensive. Others suggested a room inside of a tank of water, but if it leaked, the fireworks would be rendered useless. Meanwhile, the warehouse crumbled to the ground, and tourists began to park there during the summer season.

Each year, as the festival of the patron saint of Los Picos draws near, the widow Romeros, dressed head to toe in black, makes her way back to the town. There, she makes sure that the fireworks are properly presented by her family, then checks on the condition of San Marcos, the Saint of the Miraculously Preserved False Teeth. Each year, or so it seems to the widow, the teeth shine more brightly in the dim church, as though they possess a little fire of their own. They rest on a red velvet pillow, and a new velvet rope has been installed to keep the overzealous from touching them.

The addition of the holy object has brought more tourists to Los Picos and increased the town's revenue. Some of it has gone to restoring the Los Picos Playhouse, and this year Suárez has planned a very special play to inaugurate the new building. He hasn't decided what to do yet, but lately he's been seen talking to an old woman in a ragged dress who points at the sky a lot. She says things that mere mortals don't always understand, but Suárez, a patient man, is convinced that most things, given time, turn out for the common good.

A PEARL IN THE DESERT

oncha peeked through the shades before answering the door. A tall man in once-good clothes stood on the porch. He had called himself Mr. Trapunto on the telephone, but the greyish card he showed her through the dusty screen door said *Dr. Ernest Trapunto, Ph.D. in Musicology*. She let him in anyway.

"Mrs. Saenz?" he asked, removing his hat. Few men wore hats anymore.

"Yes," she said. "How do you do?"

"I'm very pleased to meet you," he answered.

The piano tuner had called the day before, saying that Mrs. Jensen, the parent of one of Concha's students, had given him her name. Forgetting to ask the cost, Concha had agreed to have Mr. Trapunto come and tune her piano at 2:00 p.m. that day.

The white cat slid out between his feet as she opened the door, leaving her completely alone with him.

"I'm on my way to a conference in San Diego, and since this town is so close, I stopped here to visit friends for a few days, the Wagners. Do you know them?"

"No," she said, "I don't think so."

"I knew them from Boston, where I was trained at the Leibowitz Music Academy, after attending Juilliard."

He was a nice-looking man with wavy black hair going a little grey, and a rosy complexion. A few veins showed across his nose and cheeks. He looked and moved like an opera singer, and seemed too large for the small, cluttered room. He reminded Concha of an earlier time. She smelled something like cough drops as he stood blinking in the relative dark after the brilliance of the afternoon sun.

"Well," said Concha after he'd been standing there a moment, "there's the piano."

It was a beautiful, dark red mahogany studio upright, lovingly polished, with light streaks in the wood. It was Concha's most prized possession.

"Yes!" he said briskly. "We'll have to move some of this furniture in order for me to work."

He set down his tool case, took off his jacket, and pulled the claw-footed coffee table over in front of the television. Then he moved the piano bench and pulled the piano away from the wall. He talked in a booming voice.

"This is a lovely instrument, Mrs. Saenz. How long have you had it?"

"About—almost twenty years. Since the year after I married, so since 1948."

He sat down and played several chords very loudly.

"And how long since it's been tuned?" He struck the highest C and the middle C over and over.

"Well, I've never had it tuned," she said meekly. Concha was embarrassed that one of her piano students had sent him.

"I mostly teach beginners, and the books they use concentrate on the middle range. It hasn't gotten too out of tune in the middle. At least, I didn't think it had."

"Never? Never! Well, in that case, it's in remarkably good condition. However, it is very dangerous to let it go so long, especially in this dry climate. It could be completely ruined, but I'll see what I can do. Twenty years!

"Would you hand me that bag? Thank you. It's a bit dusty inside, too, so by tuning it and cleaning the felt, we will be able to improve the tone as well. It's a good piano. These Wurlitzers were really well made in those days. Where did you get it? It has an unusual exterior."

"Oh, in Los Angeles." She added, hesitating, "It was repossessed. That's how we could afford it."

"Well," said the piano tuner as he crouched beside the piano, "it's been taken care of, that's for certain."

Concha could see a hole in one of his shoes from that angle.

"None of the strings are especially worn, yet it's gotten plenty of use. You use this piano when you teach?"

"Yes, mostly. Sometimes I go to their homes, if they want me to. But I prefer that my students come here. Sometimes Janice, the Jensens' daughter, comes here."

Concha thought about the Jensens' house, that of the people who had sent the piano tuner. It was in a nice section of town, with a big piano they had bought for Janice's lessons.

"Did you tune the Jensens' piano?"

"Yes, I did. Recommended to me by the Wagners. A nice Kimball, only three years old. But you know, some of these newer pianos aren't as well made as the older ones. This piano, I think, has a nicer tone, more resonance, than the Kimball."

"I think so, too," she said quietly. She felt better.

"Usually, pianos played by a lot of different people don't sound this good. They tend to get all the nuances pounded out of them, and the felt on the hammers wears faster."

"I don't have too many students, just eight or nine. Mostly girls. They don't hit it so hard. If they're good," she added, "they go on to the real teachers, the professionals, who have recitals and everything."

"I used to give piano lessons sometimes," he said, "but the real demand is for piano tuning. Besides, it offers more flexibility. You get tied down with students."

"Yes, piano tuning is a nice thing to know." Concha didn't want to sound as though she was prying. "How long have you been doing it?"

"About eight years now, eight years. I had one of the finest teachers in the country, Dr. Leibowitz. He learned it in Germany, before he came over. The man had perfect pitch."

He tinkered with the piano some more.

"Still, I can tell when an instrument is well taken care of. You should see some of the pianos I've tuned. Water inside from setting plants on top, old sandwiches, the finishes ruined, all the ivory off the keys. People don't understand what a treasure their piano is."

"I try to take care of mine," said Concha more confidently. She sat down on the couch with the coffee table close against her knees.

"My daughter polishes the wood with oil sometimes. All of my children like it. They all play."

"These are your children here?" Trapunto straightened up to look at the photo on the television.

"Yes." She pulled the photo closer.

"Lovely daughters, lovely. And the boys too, they play?"

"Oh, yes, a little. I taught them all how to read music. But you know how busy they get with school and everything. The oldest boy is in college now, so I don't know when he gets a chance to practice, except when he's at home."

"And who are these lovely creatures?" he said, turning to a tinted picture on the wall.

Concha blushed.

"That's me," she stammered, "with my sisters. It was taken a long time ago."

"Oh," he said, comparing her with the portrait. "I see."

Trapunto returned to his piano tuning. The screen door banged softly as a hot afternoon wind came up. Almost an hour had passed.

"Yes, just a little more here. It's very difficult to keep these high notes in tune after they've been let go so long. They tend to go back to the way they've been. Strings have a memory, you know, like people. They fall into habits. But I'll come back in a month or so for a follow-up. No extra charge."

The piano tuner would come around to the front, his sleeves rolled up and sweat standing on his arms, and hit the notes loudly, much harder than Concha's pupils ever hit them. Then he would turn to the strings, pull an instrument from his canvas bag of tools, and adjust something. He repeated this over and over, sometimes striking a tuning fork to check himself. Concha sat and looked around her dark little living room. She had meant to dust before he came. Sometimes she jumped up to hit a note if he so directed.

"Twenty years in this dry climate without being tuned," he marveled again, "and in constant use by children and students. And it's quite beautiful and rare, like a pearl in the desert, or a first edition book in an attic. You're a lucky woman, Mrs. Saenz, you really are. I think we can bring it back in tune yet."

At last the piano tuner reached a point where he decided to stop. He had been playing scales for the last five minutes, interrupted by small adjustments to the strings.

"It's not perfect, but it's the best I can do for now. As I said, I'll come back in a month and retune it. Then you should really have it done again in six months, and at least once a year after that. Now you try it, see what you think. Go ahead, sit down and play something."

He pulled out the piano bench and motioned for her to sit. She did.

"Play something," he said again. She tried to think of something with a wide range.

Finally, she played a few measures by Mendelssohn. It was hard to tell, since the middle register of the piano had never really been out of tune, but she thought it sounded a little better. She ventured a few chords at the extreme ends of the keyboard.

"Yes, yes. I think it's better," she said finally.

The piano tuner stood close behind her as she played, making Concha very self-conscious.

"Yes, it's not exact, but it will continue to improve as you have it retuned. And your piano will last much longer, since the strings were made to perform best at their proper pitch."

He was gathering up tools and rolling down his sleeves as she stood up from the piano bench.

"Well, we'll see how it sounds. I know it's better. I'm sure it will be fine. Thank you."

Concha dreaded asking the amount, but she could not put it off any longer.

"How much is it for today?"

"Uh, fifty dollars," he said distractedly. "That includes the visit in one month."

Concha's heart sank as she went to get the checkbook. Fifty dollars! Her husband would be angry. She hadn't told him she was getting the piano tuned.

"You don't happen to have cash, do you?" asked the tuner suddenly. "I really would prefer cash."

"Oh, no, I don't think so," said Concha, "but I'll go see."

She went to the hall closet to look in her purse, a little alarmed at his request. Something in his tone of voice had struck her as sinister. Now he'll hit me on the head, she thought, and take my purse.

"No, I don't," she called out from the hall. "I only have fifteen dollars.

"I really don't keep much cash," she added. "I mostly write checks."

"Oh, all right," he said impatiently. "That will be fine." He had his coat on now.

Concha returned to the living room with her checkbook. "And I make it out to you? Is that okay?"

"Yes, yes, to Ernest Trapunto," and he spelled it. He was fidgeting with his tool case now, and seemed anxious to get away.

Concha signed the check carefully and tore it out. He took it, read it, and then folded it into his coat pocket.

Then, brightening suddenly, as though he had just remembered his manners, Ernest Trapunto turned and smiled at Concha.

"Thank you very much, Mrs. Saenz." He took her hand in a courtly manner, as though to kiss it.

Concha was too surprised to speak.

"It's been a pleasure doing business with you," he said.

Their eyes met, and, for a moment, Concha could see in him a young concert pianist she had once known in Mexico, his dark eyes and the gentle smile that played around his lips. He had loved her, he said, but she had turned away from his burning glances because he was seven years her junior. Not a good match, said her family. He'll never be able to support you. And he's so young. He had pressed her hand to his chest and said that he could not live without her.

Then her gaze cleared as she looked at the older man before her. Concha saw his sagging jowls and shabby clothing. He was flushed from exertion, and she realized that the pained look in his eyes meant he was desperate for a drink.

Concha averted her eyes and withdrew her hand. She did not approve of drinking and kept no liquor in the house.

"Thank you for coming," she said, and unlatched the screen door so that he would go.

He put on his hat and slowly walked away. If he had a car, she could not see where he had parked it. She did not expect him to be back in one month.

Concha rearranged the living room, pulling the table back to the center of the room. The children would soon return from school. She put her things back on top of the piano, the dolls in stiff lace dresses, the photographs, and the music books she always kept there. Then she sat down on the piano bench, scratched from the shoe buckles of little girls, and began paging through her sheet music, looking for something to play, something just right for the newly tuned piano.

Finally, from memory, she began to play a ballad she had learned in Mazatlán, a song about sleeping butterflies near lakes of silver, a song that brought back a time when she and her sisters had worn pastel dresses and laughed. Each day had been golden, and full of promise.

GHOSTWRITING FOR THE ARCHBISHOP

A blackbird lands on the sill of the open window opposite the Archbishop's desk. The Archbishop freezes as the bird regards him with one beady black eye, then the other. It advances towards him, then retreats. He wonders if it is repulsed by his smell. The Archbishop is very sensitive about smell, especially his own. The bird flies the short distance to the desk and lands on the unsigned letter that lies before the Archbishop. It regards him at closer range, its feathers iridescing like watered silk.

"Peace of Christ! Peace of Christ!" the bird shrieks suddenly, and hops across the Archbishop's desk. Finding nothing more of interest, it flies back out the window.

The Archbishop takes the bird's blessing as an omen. He signs the letter, although it is addressed to a woman he does not know, Joanna, and contains some rather questionable statements. His signature is bold but dignified and followed by a small cross.

The Archbishop schedules himself to spend one morning from 5 a.m. to 7:30 a.m. contemplating the suffering of Mary as Jesus hung from the Cross. He says a Rosary. It is a Marian Year, and an encyclical on women in the church has just been issued.

His mind wanders, and the Archbishop finally allows himself to contemplate the twelve stations of the Cross in the context of nuclear proliferation in the twentieth century. This is more familiar ground. Several employees of the Archdiocese will soon begin serving jail sentences for repeated trespassing at the Pentagon in protest of nuclear arms. Income for the Church, both from direct solicitation and from conservative, wealthy parishioners, is expected to drop substantially. The Archdiocesan Directorate is not pleased.

The cool winter sun creeps across the Archbishop's desk. It is the first time it has shown itself in days. The Archbishop wants to go skiing, but the thought only reminds him that a skiing partner and best friend was killed two months earlier in a car accident. The Archbishop prays for his friend's soul, and imagines clear, crisp blue-white slopes criss-crossed with the tracks of skiers. He hears the swift shushing noise of skis on snow, the slight heft of the poles held securely in each hand as he shifts his weight back and forth, and experiences the elated near-violence of extreme speed.

◇ ◇ ◇

As part of the ten-year anniversary celebration of his life as an Archbishop, a round of Masses and special events are scheduled throughout the Archdiocese despite the Archbishop's misgivings. The Directorate views the occasion as an appropriate time to raise money, and will encourage parishes and religious groups to make monetary gifts to the Archdiocesan Core Offices in commemoration of the Anniversary. Their organizations will, in turn, be listed in a commemorative booklet with the Archbishop's picture on the cover. The Directorate expects to raise a minimum of 1.5 million dollars around the Anniversary.

◇ ◇ ◇

The Archbishop celebrates Mass on an Indian reservation. At a potluck afterwards in the community hall, it is announced that cakes will be raffled off, and the money raised will be the tribe's gift to the Archbishop. The local parish priest is visibly embarrassed as a chocolate cream pie is waved overhead before a bunting-draped stage displaying the Archbishop's picture. The Archbishop buys two raffle tickets at two dollars apiece.

◇ ◇ ◇

A pile of short letters awaits the Archbishop on his desk:

Thank you St. Jude and Sacred Heart of Jesus for favors received.

Thank you Sacred Heart of Jesus, St. Jude and Blessed Virgin Mary for favors received.

Thanks to the Sacred Heart and St. Jude for prayers answered and requests granted.

Thank you St. Jude for watching over me during open heart surgery.

Thank you St. Jude for answering my prayer.

Thank you, Sacred Heart of Jesus and St. Jude, for your multiple blessings.

St. Jude Novena
May the Sacred Heart of Jesus be adored, glorified, lived and preserved throughout the world now and forever. Sacred Heart of Jesus, pray for us. St. Jude, worker of miracles, pray for us. St. Jude, help of the hopeless, pray for us. Hear our prayer through His Son.
Say this prayer nine times a day. Say it for nine days. Thank you St. Jude.

The Archbishop often receives letters which are actually addressed to St. Jude. Petitioners consider the Archbishop to be farther along in the chain of command, so to speak, and so better able to convey their prayers to a higher authority. He reads all of their prayers over carefully, but is unsure if he is expected to repeat the Novena to St. Jude nine times a day. This has the quality of a chain letter somehow, and it rankles him. Nevertheless, the Archbishop repeats the Novena nine times all at once so that he won't forget to do it later. Faith is a powerful thing, and the Archbishop is not one to stand in the way of a blessing.

Beneath the petitions is a letter prepared for the Archbishop's signature:

Dear Joanna,
The memory of your sweet breath lingers with me. How I long to be near you again! To touch your face and hair, to kiss those gentle lips.

Although it's only been two weeks, it feels like two years since I last saw you. The Committee met at a closed session in Baltimore and heard testimony from witnesses concerning the alleged irregularities in the Archdiocese. It seems that people don't think I spend enough time on practical matters, and that I don't make enough public appearances. I was given a list of the names, and only two belonged to the dissident faction that has caused so much trouble. Nevertheless, that's two too many for my comfort.

If only I could see you! I'm afraid I'm distracted all the time, staring off into the middle distance when the Chancellor is trying to brief me. I hope he thinks that I am lost in prayer.

Counting the days,
Love,

The Archbishop reads the letter and signs it. He wonders who Joanna is, and if he has ever met her. He assumes the correspondence with her is important, or he would not be asked to sign these letters. He has never seen a letter from Joanna, that he can recall, and wonders how she responds to these lavish and rather intimate compliments. Is she pretty? he wonders. Young? Older like himself? The Archbishop buzzes his secretary on the intercom to take the pile of signed letters from his desk, then retreats to the inner meeting room.

Oh, Joanna, he thinks. Dear, sweet Joanna. Who are you?

◊ ◊ ◊

The Archbishop contemplates the plight of the unborn. He imagines their souls all around him, like heavy, silver raindrops suspended in the atmosphere, and wonders at their will to take human form. Why should they want to join this world of sorrows, to suffer hunger and unkindness and body odor? What exactly is this right to life? Is it not also a right to death? Because everything that is born must die.

The Archbishop looks up from his desk startled by a sudden sound. Red roses fall to the thick carpeting all around him, dew still clinging to their prickly leaves. The youths at Medjugorje had cried when the tenth secret was revealed to them in their visions of the Virgin Mother. When they wrote out their revelations, the priest had taken the writings and sent them to the Vatican, where they remain deep in a locked vault. Although other of the youths' revelations have been made public, the Vatican remains silent on the tenth secret.

The Archbishop senses a presence near him, feels that he is about to see someone standing there, when the moment passes as swiftly as it came.

Father Hopewell, the Archbishop's Chancellor, enters the study and finds the roses scattered about. He thinks they have been knocked from an enameled vase that stands on a low table.

"Loretta," he calls to the secretary, "put some more water in these, will you?"

◇ ◇ ◇

Dear S.

I am in receipt of your letter dated September 6,

1988. Please forgive me for the delay in answering. I'm afraid there is a great deal of correspondence which is sent to my office, and I am not able to answer it all in a timely manner.

I appreciate your concern over the issue of homosexuals in the Church. The position of the Church is that the inclination towards homosexuality is not, in itself, a sin. Only the actual fulfilling of such impulses is considered sinful. Thus, the sacraments can be administered to an acknowledged homosexual who has confessed himself and been absolved of all sin, in the same way that all people who have been absolved may receive the sacraments. Only an unrepentant, practicing homosexual cannot in good conscience receive the sacraments.

This is an area of great concern to the Church, and one in which a great deal of prayer and compassion is needed, both for the Catholic homosexual and for the greater Church and its many members as we come to terms with these issues. There is no information available on the number of homosexual priests in the Archdiocese. The number of practicing homosexual priests is, I presume, zero, since all priests take a vow of abstinence prior to or upon ordination.

Thank you for sharing your concerns with me. I hope that you will join me in prayer for the men and women who must struggle on a daily basis with this issue, as well as their families.

May God bless and keep you.

◇ ◇ ◇

A long-forgotten waltz begins playing in the Archbishop's head, and he remembers an auburn-haired woman at a party wearing a low-cut yellow gown. A corsage of yellow roses was fastened to her wrist. She looked at him over one freckled shoulder and smiled. Clarissa? Marie? He cannot remember her name. He only knows that he had loved her in that instant more than he had ever loved anyone else, even God.

He had wanted to ask her to dance, but he was perspiring inside of his dark suit, and knew how strong his body odor was. No matter how much he bathed or perfumed himself, the smell remained, strong and dark, like rancid bear's wool. It had kept him apart all of his adult life, the ideal priest, present but separate, unsullied by the day-to-day goings on of secular lives. He had felt imprisoned by the smell, but now he sees that it has protected him from many things.

Would he have desired that woman and her shoulders the same way if she had been a man? He does not know. And it is not his place to contemplate such things. He is, after all, celibate.

◇ ◇ ◇

The Archbishop resolves once and for all to discover who the ghostwriter is, and meet him (surely it's a him) face to face. Well, not exactly meet him, perhaps, but feel free to call and ask about some of the letters. It's not that the Archbishop doesn't trust the ghostwriter. He has absolute faith that the ghostwriter knows what he's doing. That's why he signs the letters. But, for instance, the letter about gay pride in the church. Had he, the

Archbishop, actually made that statement? And of course the question, who is Joanna? A saint? A donor? A relative? Well, maybe he won't ask about Joanna at first. Maybe after they have talked a few times.

The Archbishop finds a directory and wonders who to call. He could just ask Father Hopewell, but he doubts that he'll get far. Public Information, perhaps? They seem to issue a lot of statements attributed to the Archbishop. Maybe that's where the ghostwriter works.

The Archbishop places his hand on the telephone receiver, but a rosy glow suddenly suffuses the office, and he looks out to see a magnificent sunset over the lake, the sun breaking through below a low line of clouds. He is lost in its brilliant colors, fire spreading across the waters. By the time he remembers the call, twilight is deepening to night all around him, and the offices are long past closed.

◇ ◇ ◇

The Archbishop sits at his desk before a thick document printed with many rows of numbers. It is the five-year budget projection for the Archdiocese. He has read through about one-fourth of it and is extremely bored. He knows that the Directorate will not take his comments into consideration anyway. They think that he is daft, a fool to be protected from the real world. As though the Directorate knows anything about reality.

Rising from his desk, the Archbishop walks out on the small balcony jutting out from his office and notes that it is a fine, clear day. On impulse, he climbs up on the railing and jumps.

The Archbishop glides down towards the grassy square in front of the cathedral. Raising his arms, the Archbishop finds that he can soar upward, and he passes low over the spires of the cathedral as workmen on the roof gape up at him. The Archbishop circles once and heads out over the lake. He is having a wonderful time. The sun sparkles on the waves, and the great ocean-bound freighters toot their horns. He waves and smiles in the same way that he often does from the cathedral steps after Mass on Sunday morning. Except this is better. No one can smell him at this distance.

The Archbishop is about to soar farther out over the water when he realizes that he should use this new and wonderful gift to benefit the poor. He banks and heads for the south side of the city, where tenements crouch in dark and grimy neighborhoods, blocking the sunlight from each other's windows.

The Archbishop sees a woman stringing out her wash on a tiny landing. She shades her eyes to watch him pass overhead, but otherwise does not react. He passes over several small children playing in the street, who hoot and point at the Archbishop. A boy throws a softball in his direction, which arcs towards him, then back into the street. The Archbishop waves.

Some old men on a stoop pause in their talking and stare at him; a woman pushing a baby carriage stops and points him out to her baby and toddler; an old woman in black falls to her knees clutching her crucifix. He worries that she may have hurt herself. The Archbishop smiles and waves at all of them.

The Archbishop sees two youths kicking someone who is lying on the ground. He does not wave at them, but shakes his finger instead. They watch him as though he is a flickering image on television, then return their attention to the victim. Not sure that he can land in such tight quarters as the narrow alley, the Archbishop flies on. He mutters a prayer for the unfortunate victim, hoping that it is enough. He repeats the prayer nine times.

The Archbishop takes a final turn around the cathedral before landing on the balcony and walking into his office. The railing proves to be less of an obstacle than he has expected.

Father Hopewell is standing inside, looking at him with consternation.

"Have you had a chance to read the budget yet?" he asks.

"Yes," answers the Archbishop. "I looked through it. Everything looks fine. I say we go with it."

Father Hopewell nods slightly, but doesn't look convinced. In one motion he scoops up the budget document and leaves the room.

The Archbishop sighs and sits down at his desk. He will enjoy his new gift, assuming it is permanent, but it has tired him out for the day.

The Archbishop picks up a copy of the Archdiocesan newspaper, *The Bastion*, and sees a picture of himself on the front. The picture is seven years old, but the caption says that it was taken at the recent celebration of his Tenth Anniversary. The Archbishop does not understand why they did not use a newer picture. He sniffs at his armpit distractedly, wondering if he needs another shower.

◇ ◇ ◇

Dear Joanna:

I think of you fondly in sisterly love. Your eyes light up the sky, your hips move like the swaying leaves of a tree on a summer day. Were the lake not of such solace to me, I would move my office to face in your direction.

In my solitude I remember every minute with you. In my sorrow, I recall our joy. I hunger for your touch, for the precious moments that we have together. Soon we will be together again, the three of us, all in one.

Thank you for the lovely gift. I will wear it at Easter and think of you.

The Archbishop finds the contents of these letters very mysterious. Sisterly love? Is Joanna a sister, a nun? Is Joanna like Mecca, in that one should bow in her direction six times a day? The three of us?

The Archbishop notices that the ghostwriter uses the word "hunger" a lot in his letters to Joanna. Is that what it's like to love a woman? Like hunger? Is that what sex is like? He had entered the seminary at fifteen, and other than avoiding Father O'Shaughnessy's fat hands at that time, the opportunity has never arisen.

The Archbishop wonders what the gift from Joanna is, the gift that will be worn at Easter. He will pay special attention to his vestments at that time. His stomach rumbles. The Archbishop thinks that perhaps he is in love.

◇ ◇ ◇

It is the color of ashes. The color of ashes of rose. The Archbishop knows immediately that it is from Joanna. It smells of perfume, a smell that reminds the Archbishop of bare, freckled shoulders, of Clarissa. Or was it Marie?

The Archbishop holds the letter to his face and inhales deeply. The smell fills his head, overwhelms his senses. For so many years he has held himself aloof, and now this.

The Archbishop opens the letter and reads it. He reads it again and stands. This is it. This is what he has waited for his entire life, the Holy Grail, the Tenth Secret, the Perfect Smell. He will go to her, take her in his arms in spite of the terrible burden of his odor, in spite of what the Directorate might say. The Archbishop does not care. He will declare his love to the world, and the world will weep.

He must find the ghostwriter immediately. He must find him and tell him in person. No more letters must go out in the interim. It cannot wait.

The Archbishop opens the door and steps into the outer office, where he startles the secretary, Loretta, just as she is about to place a cigarette to her lips.

"Where's the ghostwriter?" he asks. "I must see him at once."

Loretta stares at the Archbishop, then points down the hall. He proceeds in that direction at a brisk pace. Loretta shakes her head in disbelief. She has not actually seen the Archbishop in six years.

Over the strong, musky smell Loretta has come to associate with the office, and which has caused her to take up smoking, she smells another odor. The smell of roses, of essence of rose. A swoony smell, the smell of irresponsible passion and reckless love.

The Archbishop feels reckless and happy as he strides down the long corridor, past a room where the Directorate is in session, hammering out the five-year budget. He feels a lightness, an absence. The Archbishop opens an unmarked door at the end of the hall and enters a large dark room. At that moment, he realizes that he does not smell anymore. He can approach Joanna as an equal at last. The word *transubstantiation* crosses his mind, only to be replaced by a warmth which floods through his body and suffuses even his fingertips.

At the very back of the room, behind a glass partition, a single light is burning. As the Archbishop approaches, he sees an auburn-haired woman bending over my shoulder. He cannot see our faces. He has forgotten to bring the letter with him, but he understands that it does not matter anymore.

READING THE ROAD

Sister Lucy threw a sweater over her nightgown and walked out to the highway just before dawn. The sun was hidden behind the Shadow Mountains, though not for long.

Sister Lucy read tire tracks the way others read cards or tea leaves. Her grandmother had been a Pueblo Indian, and the sky, the earth, and the trees had been an open book to the old woman, telling her the past and the future. But Lucy knew that the blood of California flowed through its roads and highways, and the highway leading west went past her front door. Everything happened first in California, but not before it passed Lucy's house.

Sister Lucy examined the highway. A pair of long black streaks showed where the brakes locked up on a rig when the driver tried to avoid a stray dog. Edie Livingston's yellow mutt was fond of standing on the road at dusk and tempting fate, looking each driver in the eye as though seeking a long lost master. Sister Lucy understood the tracks to mean that she would have a visitor that day.

Crunching her way back across the gravel, broken glass, and shredded rubber that formed the highway shoulder, Lucy stood in her yard and faced west. She could see the sharp edge of shadow cast by the mountains moving rapidly towards her across the flat desert between the town of Baker and her house. She turned east just as the sun burst over the ridge, momentarily blinding her. Lucy stood there shivering, then felt the hairs rise on her neck and temples as the temperature shot upward. Her old calico cat sat on the porch at exactly the right angle to catch the heat. Sister Lucy's skin began to feel hot before her insides had stopped shivering; she imagined that's what a frozen chicken felt like when you ran hot water over it in the sink. It would be an especially hot day.

Sister Lucy went back inside and put on a green flowered skirt, a red blouse, and purple sandals. When she first started using her powers, Lucy began calling herself "Sister" as a token of her reverence for the holiness of all life, although she had no religious training. At first, she had dressed in a brown robe, but customers responded more enthusiastically to bright colors. They thought they were getting more for their money. Still, however, she wore her keys on a rope around her waist, where they banged against her hip, and a dimestore crucifix dangled from her neck.

Lucy pulled her sparse black hair back in a ribbon, then colored her eyelids peacock blue. When she squinted and stood back from the mirror, she still looked young and beautiful, but up close her face dissolved into a thousand wrinkles. She colored in the scar on her lip so that it hardly showed. Lucy completed her outfit with red plastic earrings.

Outside, she dragged her sign away from the house and set it up by the highway: "Sister Lucy, Professional

Clairvoyant Counseling." A black, somewhat Egyptian-looking eye had been painted above the word "Open."

Returning to the house, she made some instant coffee with lots of cream and sugar and sat down to wait.

It was almost eleven before a beat-up blue Mustang with a crumpled fender suddenly braked and swerved off the highway and up to the front door. Sister Lucy tried to keep the yard neat by painting rocks white along a walkway, but people were always running over them. They had even knocked over the sign a couple of times.

Sister Lucy opened the front door just as the young man was about to knock.

"Hello," she said. "I'm Sister Lucy. Did you want a consultation?"

"Uh, yeah," he said. "Why not?"

"Come in," she said, "I've been expecting you."

"Oh yeah? You see it in your crystal ball or something?"

He looked around at Sister Lucy's hubcap collection. The hubcaps were shiny as mirrors against the dark turquoise walls. Lucy picked them up from the edge of the highway and made a few extra dollars if a customer wanted one.

"No," said Lucy, seating herself in a lawnchair across the table from him. "It's just a sixth sense. You learn to see things in a different way, is all."

"Great. Then what's my name?" he said.

"I don't know," said Lucy. "Why don't you tell me?"

"Just call me Johnny."

"Alright, Johnny," said Lucy. "Have a seat."

Johnny sat heavily in the other lawnchair, shifting it so that his back was no longer to the front door. He still wore his sunglasses, and his hands and feet moved restlessly.

"Okay," he said. "So explain how this works."

"Well," said Lucy, "I'm an iridiologist. That means that I look into your eyes. The colored part of the eye is the iris, and they're different for each person, like a fingerprint. Depending on the color variations and the flecks in them, I can tell a person's past, future, or state of health. Whichever you want. The right eye mirrors the body, the left eye the soul."

"I see. Okay. So how much does this cost?"

Lucy looked at his black Grateful Dead tee shirt and the Mustang outside. "For either the past or the future, twenty-five dollars. For a complete consultation, including a color analysis and employment opportunities, I charge fifty."

"Why would anyone want to know the past?" asked Johnny.

"People who are adopted sometimes ask for that," she answered.

"Nah," said Johnny. "I ain't no orphan. I just need to know the immediate future."

"A good choice," she said. "Most people invest in the future. That's what life's all about."

He took twenty-five dollars out of his pocket and handed it to Lucy. The bills felt new between her fingers. She took the money into the bedroom and placed it in a tackle box. When she returned, Johnny had removed his sunglasses.

Sister Lucy could see right away that Johnny was bad news; it didn't take a clairvoyant to figure that out. His eyes were a muddy yellow color, wild like a dog's eyes, and he smelled like stale cigarettes. He must have just driven in from Las Vegas.

Lucy sat down and placed her hands on top of the table, leaning forward to get a good look at him. There were dark spots in his irises, more in the left than the right eye.

"I see you in a white car," she said.

"Awright!" said Johnny.

"A fast car."

"What kind?"

Her gaze flickered involuntarily to the dark Mustang outside, then focused on his face.

"I'm not sure. But a fast car, with a big engine."

"Awright..."

"With a grey—no, silver—leather interior."

"Far out," said Johnny. He settled back in the lawnchair and gripped the plastic arms. Lucy wondered if he was high, the way his pupils remained so wide.

Then, in her own mind's eye, Lucy really did see him in a white car on the highway.

"You are going very fast," she said. "It's not your car. You are with a powerful man, a dangerous man, and he is holding you against your will."

Johnny stopped squirming and stared at her. His pupils got even larger and then very small.

"That's all I can see," said Lucy, blinking and looking away, "except for whiteness. I keep seeing white. You are trying to conceal something, so I can't see the rest. That is your immediate future."

"Shit," said Johnny softly. His face looked sad for a moment, like a little boy's, then darkened.

"That's a pile of shit," said Johnny louder, leaning forward. "I want my money back, or I'll rip your ugly little earrings off." His hands clenched and unclenched on the edge of the table.

Sister Lucy got carefully to her feet. "I'll get it."

She went into her bedroom, took out the tackle box, and slipped quietly out the door to the backyard, deadbolting it with her key.

Lucy went over to Edie Livingston's trailer. Edie had the television blaring as usual and couldn't hear her knocking, but the door was open, so Lucy let herself in. Edie was in her nightgown watching a game show and drinking cola. Even living in the Mojave desert, Edie was flabby and white.

Noises were coming from inside Lucy's house.

"What's going on?" asked Edie, only slightly distracted from "The Joker's Wild."

"I don't know. This guy just freaked out."

They heard the abrupt sound of shattering glass.

"Jesus," said Edie. "What's he want?"

"Money," said Lucy, setting her tackle box down next to Edie's couch. "I told him a true thing, and he wants his money back."

"Lock the door," said Edie. "You're closer."

After a few minutes, Johnny came out the front door, squinting and sweating in the bright sunlight.

"Hey, lady!" he yelled, looking around with his hand above his eyes. "I want my money back."

He spotted the trailer and began walking towards it.

"Hey, witch lady! Are you in there?"

They could hear his labored breathing as he climbed the steps and tried the door.

"Do something," said Edie, sitting up on the couch.

"Like what?"

"I dunno," said Edie. "Call the sheriff or something."

"I don't know if that's such a good idea," said Lucy. "I don't want any trouble."

Johnny began to pound on the flimsy trailer door.

"Hey, witch! I'm serious!" he yelled.

Lucy took her earrings off and hid them in her pocket.

"Do something," said Edie again. "I don't want him breaking down my door."

"Your phone work?" asked Lucy.

"Yeah, I guess so."

Johnny began kicking the door, leaving dents they could see from inside.

Lucy called 911. Her voice faltered when she was connected with the sheriff's office and a man got on the line. What if they arrested her instead? She couldn't recall if her business license was current.

Johnny rattled the front door like a restless bear.

"Where's my money?" he yelled hoarsely.

Lucy and Edie had backed into the kitchen by now. Her dog was nowhere to be seen. Then Lucy had an idea.

"It's inside my house!" she yelled. "In the bedroom."

"Where?" asked Johnny, rattling the door again.

"Under the bed. There's a loose board, and the money's in a sock underneath."

Johnny gave the door one last kick, then headed back to Lucy's house.

"What are you talking about?" asked Edie, as Lucy crouched at the front door in order to watch Johnny's back. "Your house is solid concrete. You've got cement floors."

Lucy waved for her to be quiet as she watched Johnny cross the yard.

She waited for what seemed like one eternity, then two, counting her heartbeats. Then she pushed open the door and crossed the yard as quietly as she could, wishing she could see through walls. She held the bunch of keys in a cold, rigid grip until she reached the front door and slipped her key in the lock.

Three heartbeats later Lucy heard Johnny grab the doorknob and shake it violently.

"Goddam witch!" he screamed, and tried to bash out a window with one of Lucy's lawnchairs. She could hear Johnny reeling around the room, bashing at the hubcaps and knocking them to the floor.

Just then the sheriff's car slowed down and pulled off the highway, lights blinking but no siren. An officer with his name pinned on his pocket got out and ambled over to where Sister Lucy stood clutching her keys in both hands.

"He still here?" asked Deputy Sheriff Ruegger.

"Yeah," said Lucy, "I locked him in."

"You crazy?" asked the deputy. Lucy recognized him from when she used to bail her husband out of the county jail.

"I didn't know what to do. He threatened me. He tried to kick in Edie's door and I was afraid he'd beat us up."

They could hear him crashing around inside.

"Here's the key," said Lucy, removing the rope from her waist in order to hand the whole bundle to the deputy. "Don't break it down."

"That his car?"

"Yes," said Lucy. "At least that's the one he drove up in."

"Let's search it," said Ruegger to his partner.

It was quiet inside the house now, as if Johnny had spent his fury, or was waiting to see what they would do.

"Holy shit!" yelled the deputy. Bags of white powder glistened in the fierce sunlight.

Soon the yard was filled with flashing lights. Passing traffic slowed down to take a look. Her game show over, Edie came out to see what was going on, and her dog materialized from some bushes behind the trailer. They watched as Johnny struggled then went limp between the two deputies.

Johnny stared at Sister Lucy for a moment.

"Ma!" he yelled. His voice was cracked and tired. "Ma!"

Lucy jerked in surprise. Did he know her? She stepped forward to look into his face, but he lowered his head so she couldn't see into his eyes.

Ruegger placed his hand on Johnny's head and shoved him into the back seat of the sheriff's car. Johnny looked tired, sitting there in the back seat, but he would not look at Sister Lucy again.

Ruegger came around the front of the car and looked at Sister Lucy.

"Did you know him? I thought I heard him call you 'Ma.'"

Lucy shrugged. "I don't got any children."

She hugged herself where her lumpy ribs had been broken for being unable to get pregnant.

"You've got to be more careful who you let in," said Ruegger. "He was probably planning to meet his connection here."

Sister Lucy said nothing.

"Get a dog," said Ruegger, turning towards the car. "You got to be less trusting."

Lucy glanced over at Edie, slack-jawed in her nightgown, and her idiot dog.

"Naw," she said. "I'll be okay."

"We'll send someone over tomorrow to take a report on the damage," said Ruegger. He got into the same white sheriff's car with Johnny. Lucy's head began to buzz as she watched the car pull onto the highway, lights flashing, and proceed at great speed back to town.

One by one, the other cars left and traffic returned to normal. It was after one o'clock. The heat rose in great silky waves off the highway, making the barren mountains waver and dance on the horizon.

Lucy picked up Johnny's sunglasses from the gravel outside her front door. The left lens was broken. She went inside to start cleaning up the mess. Her bedroom would smell like Avon perfume for a long time.

◇ ◇ ◇

At dusk, Lucy crunched across the broken glass to the edge of the highway. Her sign had fallen down, but at least it wasn't broken. The heat coming off the asphalt was still intense, and the pavement seemed to writhe like a living creature.

Lucy saw the place where Johnny must have spotted her sign and swerved off the highway. The tire marks formed a perfect cross with the truck tires from the night before, the head pointing into the heart of the desert, the foot pointing west to L.A.

Lucy knew she was safe for awhile, at least until the cross wore off or was obliterated by newer signs. She went around to the back of her house where a weeping willow grew. There, in the gentle cave formed by the branches, Lucy was building a shrine to the Virgin Mary.

The plaster statue stood in the gathering dusk, partially surrounded by empty glass jars arranged in a semi-circle. Lucy was using only the 32-ounce jars that Treetop Apple Juice came in, because of the diamond pattern around the top. Lucy's husband would have ridiculed her for attempting such a thing and probably would have smashed the shrine and slapped her around for good measure, but he had disappeared a while ago. That's when she had installed the deadbolts, in case he ever decided to return. They were never meant to lock someone inside. She had bought them without inside latches because they were cheaper, and she always carried her keys.

Sister Lucy brought out the undamaged lawnchair. The other one would have to be replaced, using half the money she had earned that day. Holding Johnny's sunglasses in her lap, Lucy considered Johnny's strange behavior earlier that day, and wondered why he had called her "ma."

"I told him a true thing," she said out loud. "A real thing. I saw it."

But somehow, she didn't feel good.

Twilight deepened around her and the desert came to life with frogs and crickets. She looked at the white flecks of stars reflected in Johnny's shattered glasses and wondered what the highway would bring her next.

A car slowed on the road, cut its lights, and pulled up at the front of the house. Lucy heard footsteps on the gravel, then someone tried the door. There was no knock. A vision of whiteness, of a white car, filled Sister Lucy's head as the footsteps came around the side of the house.

THE CANARY SINGER

T rudie Mendoza's mother raised canaries. Even before she was born, Trudie listened to the trilling and chirping of the fragile yellow creatures as her mother stood and admired them. Later, as her mother tended her prized birds, Trudie played on the dusty wooden floor, picking up stray pieces of birdseed with her tiny fingers.

It was not until Trudie was close to a year old that her extraordinary gift became apparent. Upon gaining her feet for the first time, the quiet little girl broke into the most amazing concert of bubbling, trilling, soaring sound that her parents had ever heard. Even the birds fell silent.

"Madre de Dios," said her father, lowering his newspaper, "what's wrong with her?"

"Look," said her mother, "she's standing."

Trudie promptly sat down again.

Trudie's real name was Trujilia, but no one had ever called her that. The little girl had been named after her stout grandfather Trujillo, but the name never seemed to fit.

In school, classmates noticed her right away. Although she was shy with adults and her English halting, Trudie's musical laughter carried across the room and down the hall and made students in the next class smile without really knowing why. Children were drawn to her, but teachers treated her as a disruptive force.

"Sit down, Trudie," the teachers would say, "and stop whistling at the boys," they'd add, hoping to shame her into behaving.

But the children only laughed, and the little boys liked her all the more. Her skin was pale, the color of old paper roses, but her flashing teeth and soaring laughter could melt ice in a glass and carry it off on little bubbles of sound.

Trudie Mendoza sang like a bird. She could coo and strut and trill her voice until the room was filled with the sounds of canaries, of nightingales, of doves. She could sing sweet and soft, or loud and complaining like a jaybird. She could murmur a room full of the comfortable sounds of pigeons nesting for the night, or shriek like a peahen. Trudie was sensational, and as she got older, she knew it.

"Unnatural!" screamed her mother. "You're a freak of nature. It's not right to be that way."

"But I am this way. I'm a singer!" Trudie screamed back.

"So sing! But not like that. Not like a bird. Who do you think you are?"

"I'm me!" Trudie screamed, rattling the windows. "I'm going on the 'The Ed Sullivan Show' someday!"

"Keep up the way you're going and you'll end up in juvenile hall, or worse, a freak show!" her mother yelled back. "God made me your mother, and I'll make you obey!"

During these arguments, Trudie's father, buried under his paper in the farthest corner of the house, had trouble telling their voices apart, and considered the possibility that Trudie's vocal abilities were inherited. No matter how heated the argument, Trudie's father never interfered. Even when Trudie's mother applied the leather belt to her daughter's pale yellow skin, he said nothing, though afterwards, his wife would berate him for not taking her side.

"You wait and see," she'd say. "It's not proper for a young girl to act like that. She'll run off with some no-good and do who knows what. She'll end up an actress or worse. Then what will you tell your buddies down at Kaiser Steel?"

"Déja la," he'd say. "Leave her alone. She's young."

Trudie's mother locked the independent girl in her room as a way to keep her home. When her mother took out the tooled leather belt she kept behind a door, Trudie knew she would be sore as well as confined. Trudie began leaving the house at the first sign of trouble—the quarrel at dinner, the comment about her clothes, the itchy look her mother got when things weren't going right.

At sixteen, Trudie ran away for good. She hitched a ride to Tijuana, and stayed where she could until she got a job waiting tables. It wasn't as easy to get a job singing in a club as she had thought it would be. The club owners wanted women with tequila-soaked voices and plenty of cleavage to lure the customers in. It took a lot of energy and emotion to sing the "he done me wrong" ballads that people loved, singing that ruined your voice in a few years with the rough edges and sudden bursts of volume that traditional norteño music demanded. A woman had to be able to sing over a trumpet playing right next to her, and still convey a sense of the feminine.

Skinny little Trudie didn't look the part, and she finally just started singing to an indifferent bar-owner who gave her a job two nights a week at La Rosa de Oro.

In a good week, Trudie worked two nights and was paid twenty dollars each time. The owner would count the receipts at five o'clock in the morning before deciding how much he could afford to give her. Most of her money went to the boarding house where she shared a room with another waitress. If she was lucky, they let Trudie eat a few beans and tortillas at the club, her one meal of the day. The rest of her money went to stockings, cosmetics, and second-hand clothes.

Trudie stuffed Kleenex in her bra and teetered on high spiked heels. She plucked her eyebrows into high arches, and wore false eyelashes and dark red lipstick to exaggerate her features.

She learned to smile when the men pinched her, and sometimes they gave her a dollar if she let them pat her rear end as she walked among the tables taking drink orders during her breaks.

"Tweet tweet," they'd say, puckering their lips at her. "Come over here, little birdy."

Trudie sang "Yellow Bird," which was popular at the time, and embellished it with the tropical sounds of a rain forest. She sang "La Paloma," and left everyone weeping with the reality of her loneliness and sorrow. She sang and sang, and soon the patrons chanted "Birdy,

Birdy!" and pounded their beer bottles on the tables whenever she took the tiny stage. La Rosa de Oro flourished, with a line outside every night waiting to see her.

After she began earning more, Trudie moved into an apartment near San Diego, crossing the border each evening to do her show. At first, she hardly left the apartment. Trudie luxuriated in its spaciousness and quiet after the noisy Tijuana boarding house. She couldn't ever remember having so much quiet. If she wanted, she could fill the apartment with her voice, and her voice alone.

Eventually, she ventured out for an hour or two, sometimes to shop, but mostly to take walks. After her first year as a singer, she had stopped dating customers: it caused fights, and made it too hard to leave work each night. In San Diego, she felt like a real person instead of the prize at a cockfight.

One of her favorite places to walk was the San Diego Zoo. She loved the cool green paths, the restless big cats, the begging monkeys. The zoo personnel got used to seeing Trudie in the afternoons, a little woman in big sunglasses and a bright scarf around her hair.

One afternoon she stood laughing at the toucans. They were making a rattling noise with their oversized bills which she could not imitate. The birds seemed to do it out of sheer perversity, rather than any need to communicate. Trudie was so delighted and absorbed by the colorful birds that it was a minute before she realized someone was laughing beside her.

"Look at them!" he said. "I wish I had some Fruit Loops to feed them!"

Trudie eyed him suspiciously. The birds rattled their bills again, and the man shook his head in a bad imitation. She couldn't help but smile at the pleasure he took in the tropical birds.

"My name's Joel," he offered.

"Hi," said Trudie.

"I'm a librarian," said Joel, "but Tuesday's my day off. I like to come down here and watch people watching animals, or animals watching people, or just make a lot of noise."

Trudie arched her eyebrows inquiringly at him.

"You know, libraries. We have to be QUIET!" he yelled, and the toucans turned to focus on him. A guinea fowl stopped her nearby scratching to regard Joel with first one eye, then the other. Then the toucans all rattled their beaks in unison, as though scolding him, and Joel and Trudie both burst out laughing again.

On subsequent Tuesdays, Trudie saw Joel at the zoo, and eventually they became friends. Joel knew the words to all the old movie musicals, and would sing them to animals that looked especially sad. He convinced Trudie to visit the branch library where he worked. She couldn't remember the last time she had been in a library, if ever, but the building was cool and inviting, and Trudie could size up the latest fashions in the women's magazines.

Sometimes, at the zoo, Joel would buy a postcard or a memento, "for a friend," he said, so Trudie, a little sadly, assumed that he was married or in love. He never talked about his friend, but she saw him bring some architectural books into the library one day when she arrived at the same time he did.

◇ ◇ ◇

Eventually, Trudie got booked into a club in San Diego. She hesitated, but finally asked Joel to come see her.

"And," she added, "bring your friend."

"I wish I could," Joel said carefully, "but my friend is very sick and can't leave the house. But I'll be there."

It made Trudie feel even worse, that she was jealous of someone who was sick, but she was too excited about her opening to think about it. True to his word, Joel came to see her on opening night at The Junkanoo. At the break, he whistled and stomped as loudly as the rest of them.

Afterwards, he came up and took her hand softly.

"I never knew!" he said. "You didn't tell me you were Birdy!"

"I know," she answered, her eyes shining. "I didn't tell you on purpose."

"Why? Didn't you trust me?" he asked.

"I was afraid you'd laugh at me."

Joel smiled and kissed her on the cheek.

"I think you're wonderful," he said. "And I would think so no matter what you did. Thank you for inviting me."

Trudie's contract at The Junkanoo was extended, and her act became more elaborate. The curtain opened on a stage full of flowers and greenery, and Birdy rose up in the middle of a fountain with colored lights playing on it. She sang "Yellow Bird," then there were bright explosions of light, a clap of thunder, and she launched into a fast *South Pacific* song. Dancers in Hawaiian dress hula'd all over the stage while Birdy sang and whistled and warbled like mad.

Sometimes Joel went and sat in the audience, laughing and crying at the same time. People loved it. They clapped their hands in unison at the end of her show and chanted, "Birdy, Birdy," until she came out and sang an encore, such as "Just a Bird in a Gilded Cage."

Trudie occasionally met Joel in restaurants, and although she usually wore her dark glasses and scarf, people were starting to recognize her.

"Trudie," said Joel one evening. "I have something special to ask you."

Trudie stopped drinking her iced tea and regarded him carefully.

"My friend wants to meet you."

Trudie let out a little sigh of exasperation.

"His name is Mike," continued Joel.

Trudie stopped breathing.

"He's very ill, but he'd love to meet you. I know this sounds stupid, but you've provided him, and me, with a lot of joy. It would mean a lot to him."

Trudie didn't know what to wear to visit Mike. She left her scarf off, however, since he already knew who she was. Finally she decided on a bright red dress, in case he couldn't see too well, or to cheer him up, or something.

It was much worse than she had expected. Trudie had imagined an older man in a smoking jacket, propped up with pillows. Instead, she was confronted by a young man in a black tee shirt and jeans. Mike was so thin that he looked about twelve, but his voice was that of an old man. He, too, wore sunglasses indoors, and a baseball cap over his bald head.

Mike had been an architect, and had worked at home until quite recently. Now he was too weak, and although he was sitting in a chair, Trudie got the impression that he had been carried there. He asked her a couple of questions and smiled weakly, until Trudie began to turn into Birdy in an effort to liven things up. She gabbed for forty-five minutes before Joel asked her to sing "Let's All Sing like the Birdies Sing." It was a strange rendition, the three of them singing or croaking along.

"Thanks," whispered Joel as he let her out. "That's the most fun he's had in ages."

Trudie went home and rocked herself in a blanket for a long time before she could bear to get up and get ready for work.

When Mike died about three months later, Trudie and Joel sat in their favorite restaurant until early into the next morning. Joel drank a lot of Scotch, which wasn't usual for him.

"How," Trudie finally asked, "How could you do it? Take care of him, I mean?"

Joel looked down for awhile. "Well," he finally said, "what are friends for?"

Trudie's hands began to tremble on the table. But she cupped them around Joel's hands, and looked at him first with one shining eye, and then the other.

The next time Trudie had a contract to sign with a club, she brought it to Joel to review. After three or four times that he suggested changes and she got them, Trudie convinced Joel to quit his job at the library and become her manager. It meant giving up a city employee's pension, but Joel decided that it was worth the risk.

Shortly after that, Joel got her booked into a jazz club in New York, the High Note. It was just for one weekend, but he felt that the exposure would help her career. All during the long plane ride, Trudie was apprehensive.

"What if they just laugh at me?" she asked. "A lot of people think what I do is pretty tacky."

"Don't be silly," said Joel. "People in the east are sophisticated. There's a long tradition of female vocalists with unusual voices. Edith Piaf. Ursula Dudziak. Yma Sumac. Flora Purím."

"My favorite," said Trudie. "I want to be like her, only, myself."

At the High Note, the club manager, who was very tall, looked down on Trudie as though from an even greater height.

"Yellow, huh?" he said, remarking on her ruffly dress. "Most women with your coloring don't look too good in yellow."

Trudie started to say something back when her cue came to go out on stage, and Joel gave her a little shove.

As soon as she was out there, she knew it was all wrong. Usually when she started singing "Yellow Bird," the audience relaxed and began to nod along with the familiar melody. This audience regarded her coldly, and many continued to talk or turned their backs on her completely. They were very well dressed, the women in long dresses and the men in suits, and Trudie began to feel that her bright yellow dress and the green plastic bangles lining both arms, not to mention the bright red flowers behind each ear, looked cheap. She didn't have special effects to back her up at this club, so she just sang her songs and got off the stage.

Before they got on the plane on Sunday, Joel bought all the papers. Usually he read her the reviews, but this time he read the entertainment section silently as they recrossed the country. Trudie's feelings had been right. The critics had not liked her.

Trudie stared out of the airplane window and wondered what it would feel like to stick out your hands, tuck your legs up against your belly, and feel the feathers flex and straighten along the backs of your arms as they carried you across the air currents. She looked down upon the fluffy clouds and tiny farm fields settled like quilts upon the countryside and thought how different life must be for a wild bird. She wouldn't like to sleep outside at night. She would be afraid, especially if she couldn't see in the dark.

Trudie remembered her mother covering the canary cages at night, wishing each of the little birds sweet dreams. Trudie used to make a tent over her bed out of blankets, imagine herself as a canary inside its cage, and wish herself sweet dreams.

"You know," she said to Joel, "I never did get to go on 'The Ed Sullivan Show.'"

◇ ◇ ◇

Six years after Trudie left home, she performed in the Tiki Room at Disneyland. It was a show that made Birdy proud. She came out in a long Hawaiian print dress and sang romantic songs to the accompaniment of slide guitars and ukuleles. Suddenly, all the carved heads on the walls started talking and singing, and Birdy sang right along with them.

Then there was a clap of thunder and lightning, followed by a dark, hushed moment before a spot came on Birdy and she stood way up on a platform singing "Yellow Bird," with hundreds of white doves flying around in a yellow light. The birds fluttered around for a minute over the audience before flying out the windows.

Afterwards, people mobbed Birdy for her autograph. Almost half an hour after the end of the show, Birdy's cousin Dora pressed forward into her arms, clutching a picture of her from a glossy magazine. In the picture, she was standing on a stage wearing a long, silky, yellow dress. It was slit to show off her legs, and she held a microphone between blood red talons.

Birdy Trujillo, the Canary Singer, has taken Hollywood by storm, said the caption. *Her lilting, outrageously sexy voice with its south of the border smolder has caught the attention of some of Glitter City's top stars and agents.*

Birdy blushed engagingly before signing the picture for Dora.

"This is my friend and agent Joel," said Birdy, nodding over her shoulder to where he stood by the door.

"Nice to meet you," said Dora. She turned back to Birdy.

"It's been a long time. We wondered what had happened to you until I found this picture."

"Oh, I've been busy," said Birdy. "Just getting along. How are they?" she asked. "My parents?"

"They're the same," answered Dora. "Same house, same life. You know."

"Yeah, I guess I do," said Birdy.

"Don't be such a stranger," said Dora. "Come see the old neighborhood some time."

That Christmas, Birdy sent a dozen yellow roses to her parents. Later, she sent tickets to her new show that had opened at one of the big theaters in downtown Los Angeles, but she never saw them there.

By now, Birdy was writing a lot of her own music, often songs without words. She allowed her voice to soar through the heavens, then land in short bursts upon the rocky ground. She took her audiences on adventures of flight with her, enhanced by special lighting and visual effects.

"Relaxxxx," she would say, "and let me take you on a flight of fancy...."

Without words, Birdy made them recall the good and bad in their lives. While Birdy's voice trilled and soared, a woman at the front would remember picking apples with her older brother when she was a little girl, while a man farther back thought of his first bicycle. The next moment, as Birdy cooed softly, the woman wept over a lost love, and the man remembered the time he didn't make the team.

Birdy always left her audience with the assurance that they could overcome all obstacles, that this beautiful sound, this feeling of floating euphoria induced by her voice, was her personal gift to them.

At the end of the show, as the lights slowly came up, the men and women would gradually become aware of the tables and chairs around them. There were yellow paper roses on the tables to take as souvenirs. People left her shows beaming, clutching the flowers in their hands, changed somehow by the experience. It became impossible to get tickets without reservations months in advance.

After she left the stage, Birdy would collapse backstage in a near faint. Her hands would tremble and her eyelids flutter until cool water and soothing words brought her back.

It was at this time that Birdy got an envelope full of bounced checks back from the bank.

When Joel investigated, he found that an accountant working for the show had been embezzling money for over two years. There was evidence that the theater management had been involved in the swindle, and the show was cancelled in a flurry of lawsuits and countersuits.

In the ensuing publicity, it came out that Birdy shared a home with her manager, Joel, and there was much speculation as to their relationship. Birdy, however, refused to ever comment on it in public.

"It's my business," she would say, looking a reporter squarely in the eye. "I share all of my music with the world, but I need a private corner for myself."

Because she had an exclusive contract with the theater, Birdy didn't perform for almost a year, and she was frantic for lack of activity.

"Calm down," Joel told her. "All this will get sorted out in the long run."

"But I don't have a long run," said Birdy. "I just have now."

"That's all anyone has," said Joel after awhile. "There's now, and then in twenty minutes there's now, and maybe in a year there's now."

"So?"

"So do something else right now. You can go back to your stage shows when all this blows over. Go make a movie or something."

So Birdy made a movie, *Paradise*, that would have made both Carmen Miranda and Esther Williams jealous. It included a scene where Birdy stood waist deep in a turquoise-blue lagoon and sang a duet with a dolphin. It was hard to tell which of them was singing which part. The movie didn't have much of a plot, but people loved it anyway. Birdy had taken her audience from the stage show and succeeded in getting them to the movie theaters to see her.

Birdy also recorded a few albums, something she had never had time for before. They were jazz of a sort, but her own special brand. *Birdy in Birdland* went platinum, and Birdy was hailed as a pioneer in the use of the human voice.

When the lawsuits were settled in Birdy's favor, it made the trade headlines. While Birdy was free of her contract, there wasn't enough money left after paying the lawyers to consider it a financial victory.

But Birdy claimed it had all been for the good.

"If they hadn't taken my money and closed my show," she told Joel, "I never would have started making movies. All they really did was give my career a boost."

Birdy held hands in public with Joel now, and a rumor started that the two of them would marry now that the suit was settled. When asked, Birdy would just smile and say, "I'm very happy with the way things are right now."

But her heart still felt tight inside of her, a tightness she could not remember ever not having. Sometimes she couldn't decide if she was happier when she was alone, or with somebody. Instead of dwelling on it, Birdy would go to the piano and pick out swoops and trills until a new composition began to take shape.

◇ ◇ ◇

Dora wrote to her when her mother died, and Birdy sent a huge bouquet of roses to the funeral. She was in Europe recording a program for Belgian television.

When her father died less than a year later, a lawyer sent Birdy a copy of the will that left her the house in Riverside.

Late one afternoon, a sleek yellow car pulled up to the curb in front of the tiny house. Birdy and Joel got out and went up the cracked cement walk to the front door. The grass was yellow and dry.

Birdy did not want to go in.

"Leave the door open," she said to Joel as he came in behind her. He glanced around once and returned to the car.

Inside, Birdy found things stacked in boxes, chairs piled together, the television set standing a lonely guard in the living room. She peered into the grimy kitchen and backed out. Then she opened the old hassock and found her own picture. It was the one she had signed for Dora ages ago. Under it were magazines, newspaper advertisements, a photo of her in junior high school, a picture she had drawn as a child. She closed the hassock and stepped into the little room, hardly more than a porch, where the canaries had been kept. A couple of empty cages were stacked in a corner, their doors hanging open like beckoning hands. Kneeling on the floor with difficulty, careful of her high heels, Birdy picked up a tiny feather with her long nails.

The sound she made wasn't like a canary, or a pigeon, or a nightingale. She didn't sound like a famous singer. The sound she made was soft and low and slightly grating. Birdy sounded like a middle-aged woman crying.

Birdy felt a stirring inside herself, beating and fluttering like many wings. She felt something rise up through her throat and leave her body, rise up, up through the narrow chimney and burst free over the rooftops, beating swift and sure and filled with the voice of a thousand voices before it dispersed itself over the whole city, the whole world.

When Birdy looked around again, the house no longer seemed the dreary prison she had remembered from her childhood. The windows and doors needed paint, but they were only windows and doors. The leather belt kept behind the kitchen door was missing. Birdy could hardly recall the desperate feelings that had driven her from this place. She felt a lightness, a buoyancy of spirit that comes only with time.

Birdy emerged from the house, carrying some old pictures of herself.

"You're crying," said Joel as she got in the car. Joel no longer had much strength, and at forty-six, looked closer to sixty. Birdy had learned how to drive the previous year and now drove them everywhere.

"It's okay," she said. "I'm fine now."

Joel leaned over and kissed her gently on the lips.

"Yes you are," he said.

Birdy had not latched the screen door of the house. It swung slowly open as they drove away.

FLORA'S COMPLAINT

O ne sunny morning, Flora Morales stepped out her back door to water the potted plants. It was another blazing Southern California day, and if she waited any longer, the plants would wilt in the heat. Flora sensed a shadow overhead. Shading her eyes to look up, Flora saw a dark shape looming closer and closer out of the sky. It looked like an airplane headed for the house.

"No!" she yelled. "Oh, no!" and she ran back inside, where her startled husband was watching television.

"A plane!" she yelled. "It's going to crash!"

They both ran outside to find the largest, blackest bird either of them had ever seen sitting placidly in the little fountain Flora's husband had installed earlier that summer. It was a swan, so big that it covered every inch of water on the surface of the decorative fountain. It was so black that it seemed to absorb light, and made the flowers around it appear pale.

At first Flora was frightened by the bird's size, but it remained still, quietly dipping its red-tipped bill and preening its feathers. She stepped a little closer. It gave off a smell like burnt wood.

Flora's husband brought a piece of bread from the kitchen and tried to feed it, but as he approached, the swan rose majestically and flew away over the treetops.

The next morning the swan was in the yard again, and every morning after that. The neighbors came to peer over the fence at the strange sight, wondering from what exotic estate it might have wandered. But it rose up in an unearthly swirl of wind when others approached. Only Flora could get near enough to feed it, and it followed her like a puppy if no one else was around.

At first, Flora thought that someone might come from a zoo or an amusement park to claim the swan, but no one ever did. Each night it flew away, but was always there in the morning. Its origin remained a mystery, as deep as the black shadows cast by its outstretched wings, or the look in the depths of its smoldering red eye.

Flora took her lawnchair into the backyard in the cool evenings and watched the beautiful bird as it paddled and preened, or regarded her calmly first with one blood-red eye, then the other. It made Flora's mouth set in a straight line of satisfaction.

Her family was afraid of the swan and stayed away from it. The burnt smell was always there, but Flora declared that it came from flying low over chimneys.

One day Flora found a neighbor's child lolling on the grass in the shadow of the black swan. The swan sat contentedly with its feet and wings tucked up. Flora ran forward clapping her hands at them, then pulled the sleepy child to his feet and shook him fiercely.

"Don't go near the swan. It might hurt you."

The black swan took flight over the rooftops.

After that, Flora watched the swan more carefully to make sure that no one got closer to it than she did.

One evening, while her husband was inside watching the season premieres on television, Flora began to talk to the swan in a way that she had never talked to anyone before.

"My life has been so hard," she began. "I have suffered so much, and no one really appreciates me."

She stared at her hands after this confession, but the swan didn't seem to mind. It sat serenely on the grass a few feet away, regarding her through half-closed eyes. Flora ventured to say more.

"I have raised ungrateful children," she continued. "Although I did everything in my power to make them decent, law-abiding citizens, none of them turned out right. My daughters married insolent young men with no respect for their elders, and my sons all married fallen women." Flora paused.

"They wear makeup," she said with distaste, "and let my granddaughters wear pants and play boys' games. The girls should learn how to cook and take care of dolls. I've tried to be friendly to those hussies, but I can tell that they don't care. All they care about is worldly goods, yet they never give me anything that's worth much, after all I've done for them.

"My daughters were never any good. I watched their every move to make sure that they grew up properly. I always punished them when they used slang or acted like boys. And yet they complained when I gave more meat to my sons so that they would grow up stronger. Men want wives who are submissive. I tried to make every one of the girls have a simple, pious spirit. Feminine. That's what men want."

The black swan shifted on the grass. The dim light from the back porch made its long shadow blend with those of the whispering flowers.

"And yet they acted like they couldn't wait to leave the house. Instead of praying in their spare time and embroidering pillowcases for their dowries, they bit their nails and pulled out their eyelashes. They acted as though I was trying to hurt them on purpose when I punished them, instead of realizing it was for their own good."

Flora hitched at her lawnchair and sighed bitterly. "Sometimes they didn't even have the decency to cover up the bruises.

"One of my daughters is even unmarried and," here she paused with embarrassment, "living alone.

"When I couldn't reach her at home one evening, she got upset because I called the police. I only have her welfare in mind."

Flora sighed again. "Decent people are home by ten. I don't know who she thinks she is."

The swan seemed to nod its head in sympathy.

"Even the pastor at my old church didn't understand. He actually had the nerve to take me aside and say that some of the women, he wouldn't give me their names, had complained because I suggested that they hadn't been married nine months before their first babies were born. How dare they say anything to him, when I was just letting them know that other Christians were watching them? He said that it wasn't any of my business. If he had done his job, I wouldn't have to count.

"And then," here Flora lowered her voice to a whisper, "he had the nerve to suggest that I had..." Flora searched for the right phrasing "...improperly touched some of the children. Who does he think he is? And who could have told him?"

By now Flora was trembling with indignation. "Imagine that man calling himself a minister of God. That's when I started going to another church."

Flora's voice turned mournful.

"He had the nerve to say, before I left, that I suffered from a sickness of the soul, and need help. Me!" she said, leaning towards the swan, "I who have spent every waking moment trying to enforce God's will!"

The swan ruffled and smoothed its shiny feathers.

"In fact," she added, "if I were a government official, I could make people obey the laws of God." She pondered that thought with pleasure, drumming her fingers on the aluminum arms of her chair.

"Sometimes," she said, "it's hard to see the justice in life. But I know that God has a plan."

The black swan seemed to listen patiently and attentively, resting its bill on its puffy breast as she recited her lamentations. Afterwards, Flora folded her lawnchair against a palm tree and entered the house with a great sense of calm, as though in spite of all she knew, the world was working as it should.

The years passed, and the swan became a fixture in the Morales' backyard. Flora's husband continued to tend the flowers, but retreated to his tool shed whenever the swan came too near, as much to avoid Flora's displeasure as to avoid that fearsome beak. As a result, the formerly manicured garden began to look shaggy.

Flora got old, and prepared to meet her reward. She had lived a long life, and was looking forward to her eternal rest. Her children were called together from their homes all over the country. They arrived one by one at her deathbed, and Flora surveyed them with a form of satisfaction. Only one was missing.

"I have lived a good life," she said to them, "I have never tasted alcohol or touched a cigarette. I have never been in a place where people engage in immoral dancing, or handled a deck of cards. I have never even thought an improper word, or been alone with any man other than my husband."

Mr. Morales looked at his feet and shuffled them on the floor, clearing his throat.

"Because of the pain of raising ungrateful children," Flora continued in a strong voice, "I have suffered long and deep. I count each hardship as a star in my crown. On Judgment Day, which is soon if we can tell by the state of the world, the gold will be separated from the dross, and I will receive my just reward. As will you," she said, glaring at each one of her grown children in turn.

At that, the last daughter arrived. Flora sat up in bed, pointing, and yelled, "That dress is too short!" before she fell back dead.

◇ ◇ ◇

When Flora opened her eyes, she was lying on a hard garden bench, her purse clutched tightly over her chest. She blinked at the unfamiliar light, not recognizing the overgrown flowerbeds, or the sharp-smelling hedges at her side.

Flora sat up, trying to recall what had happened. She had been sick, she remembered that, so sick they did not think she would live. Her sons and daughters had been called, arrangements had been made....

It was deadly quiet, except for the droning of insects in the overblown roses and the hedges that stretched out before her. Her feet seemed to rest on firm ground, in her same sensible navy-blue shoes, but the sky above her was a hazy, milky white, the look of late afternoon in late summer. Flora was afraid, and began to cry quietly.

Suddenly, Flora heard a raucous noise to her left and turned to confront a looming black shape.

It was her beloved swan. Flora reached out her hand to stroke it, but the swan bit her hand sharply. With a cry she jumped up, but the swan remained where it sat on the warm sidewalk. Shaken, Flora began to walk away. The swan followed at a distance, keeping one red eye or the other on her every step.

When they came to a listless fountain with a wide, low edge, and green moss growing in its cracks, Flora sat down and turned to the swan.

"Remember your fountain?" she said. "Remember how much you used to like it when we turned the hose on for you?" She splashed her hand invitingly in the tepid water, but the swan remained apart, watching her gravely.

Flora got up and began to walk again, a growing disquiet within her, but she tried to look unconcerned, fanning her hand out a little at her side so that it would dry.

After a time, they came to another fountain with benches, and Flora could make out two women sitting at the far end, talking. They wore luminous robes. As she drew closer, Flora's heart leaped as she saw her dead sister Julia, talking to a woman she faintly recognized.

"Julia?" she said uncertainly, walking up to them.

"Flora!" the woman exclaimed, and stood up and embraced her. Tears of joy streamed down their faces, for it had been many years since Julia had succumbed to cancer and passed on.

"This is la Señorita Barajas, Flora. You remember her?"

"Oh yes, Señorita. How do you do?" she said politely, and la Señorita Barajas, a tiny, white-haired woman, stood up and gave Flora one of her perfectly gloved hands before pecking her lightly on the cheek.

As they calmed down, Flora turned to her sister and finally asked: "Well?"

"Well what?" asked Julia.

"Is this it?"

Julia took in her breath sharply. "What do you mean, is this it?"

Flora began again, not understanding the look in Julia's eyes. "Is this what it's all like?"

Julia was stunned. "What do you mean? What more could you want?"

She was about to say more, but faltered as the black swan stepped up to them. It stood a little too close, and regarded them each in turn with its glittering eye.

As Flora's expression turned to terror, Julia's face softened to pity. She saw Flora's clothing for the first time.

"It is different for each of us," she finally said. "We each find what we have looked for in life."

"But," said Flora, "I didn't look for the swan! It just came to me, while I was still alive! Why is it here? I don't understand!"

By now, the two women were moving away from Flora, the swan standing between her and them. They looked back when she called to them, but did not try to answer her questions.

"We will see you again soon, Flora," her sister called out, "but we must go now."

When she tried to follow, the swan rose up on its toes, unfurled its huge black wings, and hissed in her face. Flora was really afraid of it now, and sat down on a bench and cried for some time, pulling Kleenex from her purse where she always kept a plentiful supply.

She must have fallen asleep, because Flora found herself stretched out on the chipping, wrought-iron bench. When she sat up, she was alone, but felt that she was being watched from a distance. The sky was still a milky white, and the light still that of late afternoon in August or September. Flora knew that she would find other people, other relatives, but that her shame would be almost too much to bear. The black swan would be with her always.

Flora got up, straightened her dress, and began to walk through the endless garden.

TAKING INVENTORY

Pastels seemed to be out, except for children.

Leopold Capital stood in the showroom of his business in downtown Los Angeles. He was trying to decide which models to continue carrying, and which had gone out of fashion. The brushed stainless steel models, as well as the natural woods, were doing well.

Capital Funeral Home was a thriving business, and Leopold made sure it stayed that way. He worked long hours, sometimes seven days a week, and seemed to go home only to change his custom-made dark suits. Although in his late sixties, Leopold despaired of finding a worthy successor to take over the business. His employees were lazy, and his grown son was only interested in collecting stamps. Tapping a silver pencil against his prominent front teeth, Leopold quickly wrote down model numbers on a clipboard he was carrying. He wanted to finish before the mortuary began its business day, and didn't have much time.

The door to the lobby opened, and a woman called his name. "Señor Capilla?"

Leopold looked up, startled and irritated. He had changed his name from Capilla ten years earlier in order to expand his business, and it had worked.

A young woman in a pink summer dress stood in the doorway.

"Can't you see that I'm busy? One of my assistants will be happy to take care of you in the front office."

"No," she said, shutting the glass door behind her. "I need to talk to you. I came to see about some arrangements."

"Oh? Well, perhaps we should go to my office, where we can be seated."

"No, no," she said, walking towards him. She was perhaps nineteen or twenty, and dressed very lightly for the cool weather. "I just had a few general questions. I'll only take a minute of your time, if you don't mind."

"Not at all," said Leopold. He laid his clipboard aside and stood with his hands folded, waiting. Her parents, he thought, and she's the oldest child. The dress looked cheap. He glanced down. Cheap shoes, too.

"Señor Capilla," she said. "Is it true that you survived the Revolution of 1910?"

Again Leopold was taken aback.

"In Mexico? Why, yes," he answered. "But that was a long time ago. I was just a boy." There's Capilla again, he thought. She must have gotten my name from someone I've known a long time.

"But you survived," she persisted, "and came north. And got a job as a gravedigger."

He stiffened at the term. "A mortuary assistant. That is correct." Was it someone he had known that long? "Who gave you my name?"

"The Army," she said, turning and walking along a

row of coffins. She had long black hair held back with white barrettes.

"The Army?"

"Didn't you serve in World War II, and weren't you a medic in France?"

"Yes." A memory stirred in Leopold's mind. "Frank? Was it Frank Medina?"

"No, Frank didn't make it."

"Oh, that's right...."

"But you learned English in the Army, and came home to start your business and marry Sofía Vargas." She trailed her hand across an ivory coffin lid that was carved with the likeness of an angel.

"Yes. So beautiful." Leopold remembered a coy young woman, marcelled curls, holding an embroidered hand-kerchief close to her face. His memories, so carefully held in check all these years, came flooding back.

"We have a son," he said finally. "A good boy."

"But you lost a daughter at birth." The young woman came to stand next to him. "And Sofía lost her mind."

His beautiful memory was replaced by a picture of Sofía in her bathrobe, smelling of urine, sitting and staring out the front window. Rage welled up in Leopold.

"You have no business!" he spat out. His protruding brown eyes grew hard as he whirled on her like a crow.

"There's nothing wrong with her. Who are you, any-way?" He saw no family resemblances, although she possessed an air of familiarity.

"But it *is* my business," she answered softly, "and I must be absolutely sure before I take someone."

She waited as Leopold stood trembling with anger, and as it dawned on him who she might be.

"You?" he said incredulously. "So young?"

"It is only an appearance," she answered.

"Has my own time come?" he asked.

"Yes. Time is flowing quickly. You must follow me." The young woman turned to go.

Leopold stood and looked after her with disdain. Who did she think she was, ordering the president and chief executive officer of Capital Funeral Home around like that? And a dress from the cheapest store in town. Is that any way for Death to dress?

Leopold looked at his hands, but they were the same. When he looked up, she was gone. The room was empty and had fallen to ruin, the floor was rotting, and the building abandoned.

Leopold went outside, and when he turned around, his building was gone. A great hole in the ground replaced it, with steps leading down, and steam rising out of it. Leopold's eyes bulged even more, but it was only a sort of subway entrance, with people gliding up and down an escalator with no steps.

He looked around, but Leopold saw nothing familiar. Silver vehicles like coffins floated overhead, and people hurried past as though he were not there.

I should have followed her, he thought. She came to lead me back.

But now it was too late. Buildings and people, night and day swirled around Leopold, who stood clutching his hands to his head, as time succeeded time into a whirlpool of eternity.

AMALIA

She first suspected that something had changed when the yellow roses began to bloom in the weeds at the edge of her porch. Amalia had never noticed the rosebush before, but she was delighted with it. Yellow was her favorite color. She began to water and coddle the roses, humming an old hymn as she worked.

"Here, Jana, you want a pretty flower?" she said to the little neighbor girl. Jana wouldn't look at the rose, only at Amalia's outstretched hand. When the girl turned and ran into her house, frightened, Amalia realized that only she could see the yellow roses.

Amalia had wondered what was going on for years, but the changes had been so small, so subtle, that there hadn't been anything she could point to with certainty.

At the old house, on Valley Avenue in East Los Angeles, nothing had changed for many years. Her brothers and sisters grew up and moved away, her parents died, one after the other, until only she and Rosetta were left. They never married, and the old house, with its musty books and broken-down furniture, was left to them.

At first, she gave piano lessons on the old upright, and Rosetta ran an old hand-cranked printing press in the living-room. This gave them a little income and kept them busy.

But as the paint began to peel on the house, and rain came through the roof and damaged the upstairs rooms, fewer and fewer students made their way past the old, drooping trees in front to study piano with Amalia. Rosetta's back got too bad to run the printing press, and they sold it to their church, the Spanish American Free Evangelical Church of the Resurrection, for sixty dollars. The two aging sisters were left alone with their father's books and the mice which began to make themselves at home in the sagging house.

They lived on crackers, eggs, and Ovaltine, and passed the time reminiscing about their younger days in Mexico and Texas, which remained brighter in their minds than the present. Once in a while, relatives would visit, bringing used clothing or strangers who they claimed were their children, but otherwise the sisters spent days uncluttered by concerns from the outside world. Amalia was happy. As guardian of the family castle, she had a purpose in life. Rosetta's back grew more crooked, but she refused to see a doctor and still smiled radiantly, even if it was at an awkward angle.

Then the neighborhood began to change. Families with more children began renting the houses, and quiet Valley Avenue was loud with the noise of lowriders at night. This did not cause them too much concern until the children began to taunt the two old women.

"¡Bruja, bruja!" they would chant, and eventually the teasing was accompanied by a small rock or two as one or the other of the two women scurried up the long walk to the warped steps of the porch. Amalia wept with fear and frustration, but not until Rosetta was knocked down one day did Amalia dare to tell her brother.

"Carlos, something terrible has happened," she began when he came on one of his monthly visits. He was tacking plastic over one of the broken windows upstairs.

"The children hurt Rosetta."

"What children? What happened?"

"I don't know. A neighbor family. They're always in the street, saying things to us, but yesterday they pushed Rosetta, and she cut her hand."

Carlos went to see his other sister, wedged behind a bookcase downstairs where the sisters now lived, surrounded by the least damaged furniture. She told him the story, and showed him her hands. Finally she even admitted that the children thought they were witches.

Carlos was outraged. He wanted to call the police, but Rosetta and Amalia were afraid that it would just go worse for them. Nothing could be done to the children, and the parents certainly didn't care. It would just be taken out on the two helpless sisters. Reluctantly, Carlos agreed.

Later that evening, Carlos described the situation to his wife, Concha.

"Well, it's no wonder," she said over her shoulder from the sink. "They go around all summer wearing three sweaters and a coat, their stockings falling down, and they never comb their hair. It's no wonder the neighbors think they're witches."

Carlos admitted that she had a point.

The family held a conference, and it was decided to sell the Valley Avenue house and use the proceeds to find the sisters a safer place to live, and help pay their expenses. As it was, each family gave what it could now and then, but it was Carlos who made sure they had groceries and paid the power bill. It was getting too hard to heat the old place, anyway.

Amalia was incensed. How could they do this to the memory of her father, the Reverend Moises Armadio, founder of over fifty churches throughout Mexico and the Southwest? Who would keep his books? How could they even think of selling the family property? She and Rosetta, of course, would refuse to move. But in the end, the choice wasn't given to them, and Rosetta, it turned out, didn't really care one way or the other. She knew she was not in a position to say. Her back grew a little more crooked, and the two sisters were moved to a duplex on Loma Street.

Some of the old books went with them, in a bookcase with anchors carved in the sides, just to help them feel at home, along with a box full of faded photographs, and the paisley scarf that had covered the piano. The piano itself was given to the church to use in Sunday School.

On Loma, things were a little better, but not much. The roof didn't leak, but the neighborhood was almost as bad. Amalia was so mad at Carlos for selling the old house that she didn't speak to him for four months. Her eyes were rimmed with red, and she sat in a straight-backed chair without moving for hours at a time. Rosetta did not bother her when she was like this, but went on about her business, moving like a gray crab with her shuffling, sideways walk. Carlos finally got Rosetta to a doctor, but she was told that an operation might or might not correct her ever-bending spine, and would certainly be very painful, if not paralyzing. Rosetta chose to keep her back as it was.

"It doesn't bother me," she said cheerfully. "If this is the way that God wants me to be, then that's the way I'll be. We all have our burdens to bear."

Just as though she carried a great rock on her right shoulder, Rosetta continued to bend more and more sharply down and to the left.

Carlos did the best that he could to keep the two sisters looking decent, but Amalia would wander vacant-eyed down the street, her purse dangling on her arm, her coat buttoned up wrong.

When she finally resumed speaking again, no one paid attention to Amalia. Her sister Rosetta would nod and smile, but often not respond to her questions. Carlos would assure her that the rest of the family was fine and that he would be back in a week, no matter what she said.

"When is my sister Ruth coming to visit?" she would ask. "I have a present for her birthday, which was two weeks ago, and I want to give it to her."

"Ruth is fine," Carlos would say. "Save the present for when she comes at Easter."

Amalia would hold the present, a necklace purchased at the five-and-dime, or found in an old purse, and sit at the window in her straight-backed chair, waiting for Easter.

When the rent was raised at Loma Street, Carlos decided to move the sisters again. He knew it was hard on them, but Amalia had already had her purse snatched once, and the street was too busy for Rosetta to cross alone. It was very hard for her to stand so stooped over and look both ways. She refused to use a cane, because she liked to have both hands free to fend off muggers or overly solicitous people. "Besides," she said, "a cane makes me feel old."

Amalia was angry again, at another move in less than three years, but this brought her to the duplex with the yellow roses. The roses appeared after they had been living on Highland Street for almost a year.

"Look!" she said, running inside with a beautiful bouquet. "Yellow roses just like my mother used to grow in San Antonio!"

Rosetta smiled and went to fetch her a vase, but when the roses had wilted after two days for lack of water, she didn't seem to notice. So Amalia enjoyed her roses by herself, moving her chair out on the narrow porch on warm summer evenings to inhale the delicious fragrance.

One day, maneuvering her chair through the screen door, Amalia was startled to find her nephew Ezekial from Mexico sitting on the steps. He was turning towards the wall, trying to light a cigarette.

"Ezekial!" she said, scandalized. "Does my sister know you smoke?"

"No," he answered, puffing calmly. "But it really doesn't concern anyone anymore."

Amalia was too shocked to say anything, so she sat down on her chair for a minute. It had been so long since she had seen her nephew, years and years, and she tried to think of why he would come.

"What brings you to visit?" she finally said. "Did the others come, too? Where is your mother?"

"I've been coming here every day for a long time," he said, sprawled out on the steps, "waiting for you to say something to me."

Amalia was mystified. "I didn't see you!" she said. "Why didn't you say something?"

"It wouldn't have made any difference," he answered languidly. "You would have thought you were hearing voices."

Amalia sat and thought some more. "And how is your family? I haven't seen your mother in years."

"I guess they're okay," said Ezekial. "I really haven't seen much of them since I died.... My brother sells Cadillacs."

He blew smoke into the air while Amalia tried to figure out what he was talking about. Finally, she remembered that he had died rather suddenly of typhoid fever almost fifteen years before. All the young girls in Chihuahua had cried at his funeral. Yet here he sat, still handsome and young, his curly brown hair pressed against the side of her duplex.

"Then how can I talk to you?" she managed to ask.

"I'm not sure," he answered. "But I noticed this street one day, and saw you outside, so I thought it would be polite to visit. We can go anywhere we want, you know."

Amalia didn't know. She sat and sat some more, but she couldn't think of anything to say. Finally, it grew too dark to see anything but the glowing tip of Ezekial's cigarette, so she took her chair and went back into the house.

After that, Ezekial came to visit once or twice a week, and Amalia would sit on the porch with him. He refused to go in the house. Eventually, other people came to visit, dear friends and relatives Amalia hadn't seen in thirty, sometimes forty-five years. She sat on the porch and discussed old times with them, the white beaches of Mazatlán, how sweet the water tasted in Los Mochis. The rosebush had grown up and practically screened off the porch from the street, and new flowers of a kind Amalia had never seen before began to appear along the walk. She tried to make sure they got enough water to sustain them through the stifling summer days, but it was hard work.

Amalia tried to get Rosetta to go out on the porch and visit, but she refused, saying she was too busy. If Amalia tried to force her, taking her by the arm, Rosetta would hang on to the doorframe and go even more crooked. Amalia was afraid to hurt her, so she stopped trying to drag her out, apologizing to the visitors for her sister.

They seemed neither surprised nor concerned. "She's just not ready yet," shrugged Estrella, a childhood friend. "When she wants to see us, she will."

That was a wonderful year for Amalia. While before she had been drawn and pale, her face grew rosy and plump with smiles. She combed her hair now, and dressed properly for her little evening porch sessions.

One night, rather late, Ezekial and Estrella showed up and asked Amalia if she wanted to visit dreams. "Come on," said Ezekial. "It only takes a few moments. It's the best way to visit your living relations."

Estrella took her by the hand, and they dropped in on her brother Carlos, tossing in his bed. They stood by

impassively as he relived a speeding ticket he had received that day on the freeway, and he woke up confused by their images mixed up with that of the California
Highway Patrolman.

They went to two or three other dreams that night
—a gardening dream, a church service, preparing food—
and they caught up on the nocturnal concerns of their
living family. After that, Amalia went along with them
now and then, just to see how everyone was getting
along.

By the next spring, Amalia was transformed. She carried herself like a young girl, and chattered happily to
her brother Carlos when he came to visit. He was relieved
that the sisters seemed to like their new home. He gave
the next-door neighbors fifteen dollars a month just to
keep an eye on them, and this meant that someone often
accompanied Amalia to the store, or got groceries for
them.

Rosetta seldom left the house now, self-conscious
about her back, and now bent so far double that she
mostly saw people's shoes, anyway. This took most of
the joy out of outdoor walks.

As Amalia grew healthier, she ate less and less. She
complained that eggs were too heavy for her, and subsisted
almost entirely on crackers and hot cinnamon tea. Her
skin was now so translucent, an egg would probably have
been visible through her stomach. Her eyes and her curly
hair shone.

That May, Amalia looked down the beautiful boule-
vard of green trees and formal gardens and knew that
this wasn't really Highland Street anymore. In fact, it

looked like Chapultepec Park, where she had visited as a child. The bushes were shaped like lions and birds, and there was even a statue of her famous ancestor, Manuel Acuña. The droning of bees was the only traffic she could hear.

"Where are we?" she asked. "I mean, really, what is this place?"

"Purgatory," answered her deceased sister Julia, "a way station to heaven."

Amalia was stunned. "But we don't believe in purgatory, do we? That's Catholic!"

"Probably not," sighed Julia. "I've never seen our father here. But it might just be that we haven't been here long enough."

"It seems long enough," said Ezekial. "What's wrong with purgatory, anyway? It's not so bad."

"No, it's not," agreed Amalia, "but our family doesn't know."

"Know what?"

"That we're in purgatory, that purgatory exists."

"You're not, really," said Ezekial to Amalia. "You just visit a lot."

"Oh, I see," said Amalia. A cool breeze blew the scent of jacaranda blossoms across the porch, with just a hint of salt air mixed in.

"Not that we blame you," added Julia. "We love to see you. And we have plenty of time on our hands."

"But we need to tell them!" said Amalia. "They should know!"

"How?" asked Julia. "They wouldn't believe us."

"No," said Amalia, "no one pays attention to what I say anymore, and I'm still alive. And they're concerned with other things, busy with their own lives. When we visit their dreams, they're full of new cars and work and the faces of children. Where did all those children come from, anyway?"

"That's what happens when you have a big family," said Julia. "Lots of nieces and nephews and second cousins. I'm sorry I never had children. Only Ruth's children were like my own."

"Ruth's children!"

An idea was coming to her. In their nighttime wanderings through the dreams of their relatives, they had come across Ruth's youngest, a young woman who lived in a part of the country where Amalia had never really been. The dreams were cool and wide, full of nights on the desert and luminous skies, rooms full of dusty books, and a fear of the color combination of pink and black.

"Rachel would believe us!" she cried, jumping up. "We can tell my niece Rachel, and she will tell the others!"

"Yes, Rachel," said Julia. "My sweet little Rachel. And she's smart, too. She'll figure out a way to tell them, and make them believe."

"Well, maybe," said Ezekial, doubtful. "Your relatives are all so stubborn," he said, as though they weren't his relatives, too, "that they may just call her a heretic and put her on a prayer list."

"Well, we must try," said Amalia firmly, "and Rachel is our only chance. We will all go to her in a dream," said Amalia. Her mind was made up now. "We will go and tell her that we are all right and we are in purgatory, and that we will see her on the Other Side."

So that's what they did, late that summer, when the last petals were falling off the yellow rosebush, Amalia and Julia and Ezekial. Amalia held Rosetta's hand through the open doorway while they dream-traveled, so she was partially included, too.

Rachel got the message, loud and clear, and waking, was impressed that she could dream so well in Spanish after all these years, for at first she thought that the dream had originated in her own mind. But the longer she thought about it, the stranger it seemed, so she got up and wrote the message down, word for vivid word, and listed everyone she could remember seeing as they stood on the porch, with that swirling garden behind them. It was hard to sleep after that, so she sat awake until the dream faded a little and she could return to her indistinct slumbers.

◇ ◇ ◇

And so, not knowing how else to tell it, I have written this story. The Indians in this part of the country, the Northwest, have a term, *sheel-shole*, which means "to thread the bead." It refers to a way of traveling from inland to the ocean by guiding a boat from one interconnected lake to the next. My aunt Amalia is still alive, but it's only a matter of time before she paddles her canoe, yellow roses and all, out into the open sea.

LA ESMERALDA

Straightening the ruffles on the curtains, she could not forget it. Stirring the soup in the kitchen while the cook waited for her to leave, she could not forget it. Sewing the torn lace back onto the hem of one of her daughter's petticoats, she could almost forget it, but Estela cringed every time she remembered the hurt, closed look on Esaías' face as she tried to talk to him.

"Papá would love for you to join him in the business," she had begun. "With five daughters, he has no one to help him, no one to accompany him on his business trips.

"You could travel," she had added, thinking this might appeal to Esaías' perverse sense of adventure. "Every year, he goes from Piedras Negras to Tampico, taking orders for thread and cotton cloth."

Esaías' silence had persisted as he continued to pack his saddle bags. Estela felt awkward, out of place standing in the supply shed next to the stables, still wearing her indoor shoes. Esaías was not yet dressed in his travel clothes, so she felt that she had time.

"I do not want to sell dry goods," he had said, finally, as he measured oats from a large sack into one of two bags that would hang on either side of the horse.

"Why can't you be like other men?" Estela had blurted out, then had run back to the main house, but not before seeing that look on his face, a mixture of hurt and stubbornness that seemed more and more to characterize their entire marriage.

A few minutes later, she heard the gate to the street open and the horse clattering away, and thought he had gone for more supplies. But upon looking in his bedroom, Estela found Esaías' town clothes abandoned on the floor, and knew that he was gone.

That was yesterday, and she had slept badly that night. Rising early to make sure that the servants began to boil water for laundry that day, Estela saw that dark shadows smudged the fair skin under her eyes.

"A widow," she thought as she pinned up her reddish-brown hair in the mirror. "I feel like a war widow, except that just when I'm used to his being gone, he comes back."

She tucked a perfumed handkerchief into her sleeve and left her quarters. A wonderful miniature carriage stood by the house in the breezeway, awaiting a second son.

She could see her two daughters in the garden, one with curly black hair, one with straight, reddish hair like her own, bent and giggling over something Estela could not see. The day was warming up, and she felt weary already. She stood with her hand pressed to the side of her face, watching them. The perfume from her handkerchief filled her head.

From the kitchen doorway, an old Indian woman watched, and saw the woman's mother in her tired eyes.

"Señora," she called. "There's good coffee here for you."

Estela swept the hair out of her eyes as she helped hang the sheets to dry, and saw a vee of cranes crossing the brilliant blue sky. They were heading northeast, towards the Gulf and fishing in abundance. She stabbed the clothespin onto the line, nearly tearing the sheet in the process. The laundry maid would rather not have had her help, and Estela knew this, but she had to keep herself busy or she felt that she would go mad.

Miguelito, her eldest child, returned from his classes at the Academy. He came out to the courtyard to greet her with a kiss.

"My papá has left?"

Estela sighed. "Yes."

She watched her son out of the corner of her eye. He had accompanied his father before on his adventures, and she worried that someday she would lose them both.

Miguelito just shrugged and removed his bookbag from his shoulder.

"I'll be at Chucho's until merienda."

Miguelito was good at school, and friends had said that the best thing for him would be to continue his studies at an American university.

She watched her tall, dark-haired boy as he walked back into the house swinging his books, and felt another pang in her heart.

Estela just had time to visit Blanca before late afternoon merienda. She changed her dress and shoes, draped a shawl over her head and shoulders, and called the maid to accompany her the two blocks to her friend's house.

Expecting a child in four more weeks, Blanca no longer went out. Instead, swathed in layers of pink silk and lace, she received friends on the cool, lemon-scented veranda of her house, where the maids brought cold manzanilla tea and freshly baked pecan cookies.

"Estela!" exclaimed Blanca from behind a sandalwood fan, as though she had not expected to see her. "How nice of you to come!"

Estela pecked her on the cheek and sat down at the white, wrought iron table. The tea tasted good.

"You look wonderful," she said.

This would be Blanca's eighth child. She would have to hire an additional woman to help care for the children.

"Thank you, Estela," said Blanca. "I would rather have cooler weather, but it won't be long now. Look what my mother-in-law gave me. Rosa?" she called to the maid. "Bring me the little confection from my mother-in-law."

The maid returned with a tiny, lace-infested dress with an overskirt of tulle.

"How can you be so sure it's a girl?" asked Estela while admiring the dress.

"After seven children, I know," said Blanca emphatically. "She floats like a little angel; she's not heavy like the boys."

This made Estela laugh. Blanca always cheered her up. Still, she could not help but feel a little envious of her friend. Estela was thirty-two years old, and had not had a child in six years. She longed for the joy that a new baby would bring.

"Esaías is gone again?" said Blanca more gently, laying her pudgy hand on her friend's thin one.

"Yes," said Estela. "I guess everybody knows."

"I can tell by your face," said Blanca. "You look so sad when he's gone."

"I want him to be happy," said Estela, "but he's so restless when he's home. Papá wants him to go into business with him. He hasn't asked his other sons-in-law. He likes Esaías. But my husband just wants to spend money on prospecting."

Estela moved the little dress away from herself so that she would not pick at it.

"Have another cookie," said Blanca, and took another herself. "You can't worry about things you can't control. Men have to be men."

"Is that right?" said Estela. She could not hide the bitterness in her voice.

"Just think. He could have a mistress and a dozen children on the side. He could be a drunkard and roar down the streets of Saltillo at all hours. That would be an embarrassment."

"For all I know, he does have a mistress," said Estela, "but I don't really think so...."

"I don't either," said Blanca. "He's had eyes only for you since we were children. Even that scary father of his couldn't keep him from courting you."

Estela smiled briefly at the memory of Esaías sitting nervously in her father's parlor while she kept him waiting.

"Papá was afraid that he would want to observe Jewish ceremonies. But he promised that we would raise the children Catholic, and we have. I think it's mostly his parents who are that way.

"I just don't understand why he has to be gone so much."

"Don't worry," said Blanca. "Men go through these phases." She laughed. "If I asked Gustavo everything that he does, he would be insulted."

Here she imitated her portly husband with her elbows out to her sides: "It's not women's business what I do. Go tend to your children. Don't I give you everything you ask for?"

Estela's eyes widened and she laughed out loud. The imitation had the ring of a real conversation, something she had not suspected between Blanca and Gustavo.

"Still," said Estela, "it seems to be getting worse instead of better."

She wanted to tell Blanca about all the money he took each time, but thought better of it. Saltillo was not a big city, and everyone knew everybody's business anyway.

Estela sipped her tea and stared moodily at the canary in its painted cage as it sang and sang, filling the fragrant garden with sound.

Estela cut the string holding together a skein of heavy thread and spread the cotton over her daughter's outstretched hands, shaking it gently to loosen the strands from each other. Then she began to wind the pure white cotton into a smooth, fat ball.

"For Christmas," she said, "for Christmas we will crochet new napkins to go with the tablecloth. I'll have

Lupita starch them until they're so stiff that they just lie there on the oak table, straight as a board, until you pick them up. Then they'll unfold like angels' wings."

Her daughter giggled and held her hands up without effort as her mother wound quickly.

"Will I get a new dress?" she asked.

"Of course, mijita," answered Estela. "Don't you always?"

Her daughter hummed to herself happily, imagining herself at midnight Mass, the whole town turned out to see her in a new sky-blue velvet dress with a white lace collar. Her sister would wear a dress very much like it, only a different color. She imagined the family, lined up in a row in church, then wondered suddenly if her father would be there.

"¿Qué piensas?" asked her mother. "What are you thinking? You look so serious."

Angelina shook her head and smiled, and concentrated on the growing ball of white in her mother's hands, dipping and raising her own hands in a rhythm to smooth the passage of thread.

◇ ◇ ◇

Esaías woke with smoke in his eyes and a weight like stone in his heart, his bones fighting the rocky ground. The campfire had burned out at least an hour earlier, and the remnants of burning coals sent a low, greasy smoke creeping along the beaten ground to where he lay tossing under a tattered wool blanket.

Coughing and rubbing his eyes, Esaías sat up in the chilly dawn and looked across sparse hills to where the cerras hunched like sleeping animals on the horizon. His horse, lightly hobbled, snorted at his stirring as she grazed on the desert weeds. He would not reach his destination for another two days.

In the intervening miles lay several promising streams, where Esaías would sample gravel beds and stream cuts with his prospecting equipment.

"Ah, the magnificent outdoors!" said Esaías without much enthusiasm as he stood and stretched in his long johns. It was deadly still except for the soft snuffling of his horse and pack mule. Twenty-four hours earlier, he had made a hasty retreat from his home in Saltillo, his wife's recriminations still echoing in his ears.

"How can you waste my father's money on this rubbish?" she had said, gesturing at a miner's pick he had just purchased at Severino's shop. It had a fine, curved head, with a blunt back to it for cracking open ore samples.

"You have everything you could want right here, yet you insist on endangering yourself in the hills. Every day there are new reports of Texas Rangers and marauding indigenous. Papá needs help in the store. Why can't you be like other men?"

Like that sniveling brother of yours? he had thought, but not said out loud.

"Why can't you be like other men?" he asked himself as he shaved by touch. "Why can't you sell women's cotton goods and go to the symphony and give your wife yet another child?" They had only three, and a man was not commonly considered macho until he had four, and at least one son. Fortunately their eldest was a son, Miguel.

Esaías buttoned his shirt, hitched up his braces and donned his coat. Whistling in low, short bursts to his animals, he flung the pack saddles over the wooden frame on his mule's back, tying them down securely. La Gata, as he called his horse for her pantherlike walking gait, stood calmly as he saddled up and mounted for the day's ride. Clamping his pipe between his teeth, Esaías swung about and headed across the sandy flatlands, west towards the Sierra Encantada.

Esaías topped a rise and looked into the Indian camp. Three children and an old man stood and stared back at him. He recognized this family. He knew that there was an old woman and a young one as well, and sometimes one or two younger men who probably worked in the mines. They seemed to wander the same area as his own, eating God knows what that they found in the desert. The man wore a long, belted shirt and no trousers. Only young men or city dwellers affected the wearing of long pants that caught in bushes, collected dirt, and impeded a runner's progress. These people carried everything they owned on their backs, and traveled many miles in a day. The children wore nothing at all. Esaías dismounted and led his horse and mule at a leisurely pace down the steep hill.

Greeting the viejo in his own language, Lagunero, Esaías seated himself by the fire where he cut off a piece from his tobacco plug and passed it to the old man. They both sat and chewed in silence while the children resumed their game of kicking a small, black ball made of some gummy substance back and forth between them. The family's dogs had caught and killed something, and growled over its small remains with pleasure.

This went on for close to three-quarters of an hour before Esaías pulled out his ore samples and began showing them to the viejo, asking him if he had seen any rocks like these, and if so, where. Esaías handled them lovingly, the red dirt from some staining his hands and nails, and set them in a semi-circle around his feet as he finished with each one.

Esaías declined the old man's offer to share their stewpot, and led his horse and mule up the other side of the gully in which they were camped.

Just as he remounted his horse, Esaías could see the two women returning to camp, carrying heavy baskets of wet clothes balanced on their heads. They had been down at the stream, washing. One looked to be in her mid-twenties and the other could be her mother, but it was hard to tell. The nomadic life gave the Indians of northern Mexico a hard, wind-blown look, and one of their women could be twenty or fifty and still have a small child clinging to her skirts. As the children ran up to the women, Esaías wondered how many of them belonged to the younger of the two.

Esaías reached the base of the next line of low-lying mountains by nightfall.

Waking early the next morning, Esaías took the time to brew a pot of coffee and open some tins of food.

"I'm getting soft," he complained to La Gata, "and so are you." She was nuzzling his gear with soft, snuffling noises.

"Each time I return to the hills, my bones find more rocks in them. But never the right kind of rocks."

He slapped the canvas bag of samples that lay beside him. The old man had pointed at a shiny black and gray rock and indicated that he had seen that before. It was Esaías' most valuable ore sample, loaded with silver and a trace of gold.

"Maybe this time," he said, "maybe this time."

Esaías relented and let the horse feed from one of the bags of oats he carried to supplement her diet of weeds and grass.

Esaías spent most of the day crossing a high, flat plain with little relief from dust or sun. The air seemed to hum with intensity. The horse sweated profusely, and Esaías wiped his own face constantly with his bandana. He had learned long ago not to remove his hat in the hot sun.

Just before dusk, he reached the village of El Socorro, and was able to have a decent meal before bedding down for the night at the outskirts of town. He was very close now, and the stars in the high, clear air seemed to line up and point the way into the Sierra Encantada.

The next day he came to a fence and gate marking the road to a mine entrance, with a sign warning that trespassers would be shot. He skirted the fence to the east until he was able to get a clear view of the entrance. Armed guards lounged about against the bare rock. It must be producing, he thought. It must have something besides lead coming out of its bowels. This was the place the old man had talked about. It was called "La Esmeralda."

Esaías kicked his horse and continued up the flank of the mountain to the high ground that produced too little for the large companies to worry about, where mountain streams brought forth the treasures of Mother Earth. He thought of his ore samples and began to hum a little tune.

"¡Andale!" he urged La Gata. "Let's find a nice little stream where you can rest all day and I can get covered with mud like a monkey."

They continued to climb upward, up, as the air turned cooler and the desert landscape gave way to scrub pine and inviting pockets of meadow. The horse and mule tried to turn away and graze, but Esaías continued upward towards the rocky high ground, a vision of black sand flecked with gold at the bottom of a crystal clear stream filling his head.

Esaías remained on the Sierra Encantada for three days. During that time, he hardly left the streambed, reaching into his gear for beef jerky and drinking directly from the running water. He sang out loud as he worked, folksongs and popular songs of the time, and delivered long speeches on the state of the economy and the moral deficiencies of modern man. La Gata took it all in with a grave air, never daring to interrupt her master.

"Ay, Gata," he said, "what is the world coming to? First the Spanish invade us, then the English and the French. All we need is a little peace and quiet so that our country can have a chance to grow up. Then the Americanos want everything. You'd think this was the land flowing with milk and honey, rather than a desert with a few saguaros and a few poor Indians.

"If I were king," and here he straightened up and groaned at the eastern horizon, "if I were king, what would I do?"

He sighed and shook his head. "I'm glad I'm not king. Or president. I can't even handle the politics of my own household."

La Gata snorted and moved a little farther away, hopping on her hobbled front legs.

"Always a critic," said Esaías. "I'll bet you couldn't handle things any better than I do." But he wasn't so sure.

Esaías wished that he could have brought Miguelito on this trip, but school had already started. Miguelito studied too much, he thought, and needed to spend more time outdoors. Esaías was afraid Estela had turned him into a mama's boy, her only son, and would probably turn him against his father as well.

At nightfall, when it became too dark to tell the lead from the gold, Esaías would fling himself down on his bedroll, exhausted, and contemplate the fiery stars overhead. He often imagined holding Estela in his arms out here, showing her the Milky Way and the Big Dipper and the meek deer in front of Orion, the mighty warrior's arrow pointed at its heart.

But he knew that she would not enjoy it. She would be afraid of coyotes and Indians, and worst of all, of what the neighbors would think. Esaías tried not to let these thoughts disturb him, but at night they came unbidden.

One night, Esaías dreamed that a fiery chariot came out of the sky, like the kind that came for the prophet Elisha. A man with a flaming beard held the reins, a man who looked like his father, only bigger, fiercer. He pointed into the black, flowing waters and disappeared in a shimmer of light. The next day, Esaías found two large nuggets at the spot.

He woke each morning with the dew on his matted hair, soaking his clothes. During that time, Esaías saw no other humans.

Towards the end of the third day, his supplies running low, Esaías packed up his gear and descended the Sierra Encantada. He had filled two small rawhide bags with nuggets—one with silver, and one with gold. He planned to cross the burning plain during the early evening hours, but barely remembered the passage.

His head throbbing with fever, Esaías gave the horse her own lead as he struggled to remain upright. Although he drank all of his water, having filled his canteen at the running stream before he left, his mouth continued to feel dry and cottony. By late evening, Esaías passed a half-mile north of El Socorro without even seeing it. He wandered into the seemingly endless line of low hills beyond, vomiting and dismounting every few miles to relieve himself due to excruciating cramps. The last thing he remembered was seeing a smoldering fire in the valley before him, and realizing that he did not know if they were friend or foe.

◇　◇　◇

Estela smoothed her fine cotton nightgown as she sat at her vanity to braid her long hair. Estela resolved that she would not cry tonight, that she would say her prayers and sleep the sleep of the righteous. In the morning, her father's lawyer would call at the house.

Ernesto Vargas came to the house the next day promptly at ten. Estela had known him since she was a little girl, but his dark, severe appearance, always in an expensive suit, a high cravat strangling his narrow neck, never ceased to startle her. She remembered that he was a distant relative of Esaías'. Nevertheless, he had handled her father's legal matters for many years, and she trusted him implicitly.

Estela sent the maid to get them coffee as Señor Vargas set his briefcase on the floor next to his perfectly shined shoes.

"Now," he said, clearing his throat. "Exactly what is it that I can do for you?"

Estela hesitated. This was going to be harder than she had thought.

"I want to restrict access to our bank account," she said. She tried to control her hands from twisting her handkerchief nervously.

"I see. Access by ... your husband?" he asked discreetly.

The coffee arrived, and they each paused to take a cup and saucer, waiting until the maid left the room before continuing.

"Yes," said Estela. "You see, Esaías recently took out twenty thousand pesos for a trip into the Sierra Encantada. He, as you may know, looks for gold. But this is the fifth time this year that he has done so. Each time, he takes a lot of money."

Señor Vargas raised his eyebrows over his coffee cup, but Estela plunged ahead.

"You see, it's not me I'm worried about," she said, "but the children. We would like to send Miguelito to college in the United States, but it is very expensive. I'm afraid all the money will be spent before he turns eighteen."

"I see," said Vargas. "This is a serious matter. But under the laws and customs of this country, you do have the right to do this. Especially since you brought most of the material wealth to this marriage."

Estela felt relieved. She had thought as much.

"Furthermore," said the lawyer, carefully setting his coffee on the low table between them, "you have just cause.

"Now, this sort of thing normally comes up," here he paused delicately and wiped his lips, "when one partner, usually the husband, is spending money on another person who is a threat to the foundation of the marriage itself."

Estela looked at her hands and blushed.

"In that case, concrete proof is usually needed in order to bar access to the family's finances.

"However," here Vargas leaned over in a somewhat consoling posture, "conspicuous waste of the joint assets on a common vice, such as drinking or gambling, is also just cause. I think that having the gold fever probably qualifies under the second set of circumstances."

Here the lawyer paused again, forcing Estela to look up and meet his gaze.

"Is this what you want?" he asked.

"Yes," she said. "Yes, it is. I have considered all my options, and prayed long and hard about it. I don't see what else I can do."

"Very well then," said Vargas, picking up his brief-case and setting it across his knees. "I will have the proper documents drawn up."

"It's not for me," she said again. "I care nothing for myself. Only let there be something left for the children."

Vargas paused in his notetaking and gazed at her over the top of the briefcase.

"I feel," he said carefully, "that you are making a wise decision. If I did not know the people involved, I might caution you to wait awhile. But in this case," here he closed the briefcase with a firm click, "it is a known fact that Esaías may well ruin the family, if left unchecked."

Estela felt as though she might faint, or cry. Instead, she drained the last of her coffee in a somewhat unladylike manner.

Vargas rose to leave. "I will have the necessary documents drawn up, and bring them by for you to sign. Once that is done, a copy will be left with your banker to ensure that your wishes are followed."

"Thank you," said Estela.

"I am at your service," said Vargas with a slight bow. "I will see myself out."

Her composure having reached its limit, Estela sat back on the velvet couch and wept.

◇ ◇ ◇

Esaías inhaled the stench of uncured hides. Opening his eyes, he found himself in a smoky interior, too dim to make anything out. His eyes would not focus. His head whirled in confusion and he felt sick to his stomach. My God, thought Esaías. I've died and gone to Hell.

He closed his eyes and dreamed strange dreams. He saw people from a world oddly like his own, yet somehow different: a woman at a piano, a sailor telling stories, a tiny yellow bird, and an old woman dressed like a gypsy bending over a strange, shining road. Esaías felt somehow that he was remembering the future, that he stood midway in a stream of time that parted and flowed on either side of him like running water.

The next time he opened his eyes, Esaías saw sunlight through chinks in the structure. When the young Indian woman pulled a blanket back from a low doorway and came to stand over him, he realized the Lagunero family had somehow found and rescued him. He closed his eyes in gratitude and rested until cool water was pressed to his lips.

Esaías slept peacefully for the rest of that day, then pulled himself up and staggered outside at dusk. The old Indian man sat by the fire smoking, and regarded him with a calm eye.

"What happened?" asked Esaías. "Where did you find me? I—I can't remember anything."

The old man waved his pipe westward. "Bad water," he said. "You got the bad water sickness. We could smell you coming."

Esaías remembered his state while crossing the desert plain, and broke into a shaky grin. He brushed back his greasy hair and sat down opposite the old man.

"I owe you my life," he said.

The old man waved his pipe again, dismissing it. Esaías noticed for the first time that the Indian had a tattoo on the back of his hand.

The next day, Esaías packed his bags and tried again to thank the old man. He knew better than to try to talk to the women, although he knew that they had tended him. They would only lower their eyes and back away from him, shaking their heads that they didn't understand, though he had been told that his Lagunero was very good.

Esaías rose early the next day and rode into Monclova, about two hours farther southeast. He stopped at a dry goods store and went inside, intending to buy a peace offering for his wife. When he spotted the roll of sky-blue cotton calico, however, Esaías realized that he wanted to give it to the family he had just left. He spent the last of his cash on the bolt of cloth, and rode back into the hills. The camp was empty when he returned, but he laid the cloth just inside of the hut, careful not to disturb the crossed sticks that had been placed there to protect their belongings from evil spirits and superstitious marauders.

◇ ◇ ◇

Estela was not prepared for the sight that greeted her when she went outside to see what all the commotion was about. His beautiful white horse caked in dried mud, Esaías looked like a scarecrow on top of the saddle. Miguelito helped his father off the horse, which was led away to be brushed and fed. Esaías smelled, and Estela covered her nose and mouth in spite of the bad example it set for the children.

"Querida," whispered Esaías as they brushed past, and the heart of stone that she had harbored for ten days melted and drowned at the touch of his hand upon hers. The document barring Esaías from further access to their cash holdings had been prepared, but Estela had put it in a drawer rather than signing it the day before. Now she saw that he had been sick, that there had been a reason for his long delay. She would nurse him back to health, slowly, and he would courteously ask her father for indoor work, due to his frail constitution.

Bathed and fed, Esaías fell into a deep slumber. He dreamed of the streambed, the rich red earth, and the salamanders he sometimes disturbed in the shallow waters. They said if you threw a salamander into a fire, two would emerge. Then he dreamed of the tattoo on the old man's hand, and realized that it, too, was a salamander.

Early the next morning, Esaías awoke to the smell of sage and leather and sweat. He opened his eyes and saw that he was in his own bedroom, dressed in a clean nightshirt. Rising and opening the window that faced onto the courtyard, he saw the servants tending a small fire. When one of them lifted a shirt with a stick and placed it in the fire, Esaías realized that they were burning his clothes.

Esaías felt renewed, reborn. For the first time in several days, he allowed himself to think of the bag of gold and the bag of silver in his possession. They rested upon the desk below the window, probably placed there by his son. Esaías drifted lightly down the passageway to where his wife slept. He sat by her side, admiring the flawless skin and the braided hair, like fire and gold, that rested upon her breast. Unable to restrain himself, he pulled back the covers and got in beside her. Half asleep, Estela pulled him to her with a small sigh.

A loud noise woke Esaías the second time that morning.

"Who was she?" screamed Estela. She sat bolt upright in the bed, twisting the blankets between her hands.

"How could you come here to my bed after lying with your, your fancy woman?"

Tears streamed down Estela's face as Esaías tried to blink himself to consciousness. He must have been talking in his sleep.

"She saved my life," he said, thinking he must have talked of the woman who had nursed him. "Nothing happened. I was sick. She was just an Indian."

"No Indian is named Esmeralda!"

"Esmeralda?"

"Esmeralda! Esmeralda! Esmeralda!" screamed Estela as she gained her knees and struck him rhythmically across the face. "Go back and squander her money on your adventures."

"La Esmeralda!" exclaimed Esaías, now fully awake and finally comprehending that he had been dreaming about the mine. He burst into helpless laughter and lay back on his wife's lace-embellished sheets.

Almost strangling with fury, Estela grabbed her robe and fled from the room. Her hand shook so that she could barely fit the tiny key into the lock of the writing desk in the study. Her hair in disarray and her robe barely concealing her nightdress, Estela sat at the desk and signed the document, the servants clucking at a disturbance so early in the morning, and so soon after the master's return to his household.

"There!" said Estela, bursting back into her own bedroom. "I've signed it! What is mine is no longer yours! Now get out! Get out!"

With surprising strength, Estela dragged Esaías from her bed and propelled him towards the door. Confused and a little insulted, Esaías shook her off and left of his own accord. She slammed the door with a mighty crash, leaving Esaías to make his way back to his own room to dress and have his first pipeful of the day. It was not until later that Esaías understood the full meaning of her malediction.

◇ ◇ ◇

Esaías urged La Gata up the steep cobblestoned street leading to the bluff above town. Up, up they went through a twisting narrow way between high, secretive walls. On the right they passed the ruins of a dwelling, abandoned over two hundred years earlier, all but the foundation carted away. Morning glories twined around the weathered stones in rampant growth.

The narrow lane opened into an ancient growth of cedars at the top of the bluff, and the streets leveled out to parallel the cliff edge.

Esaías followed a road away from the cliff that led to his father's house.

The house, set low against a slight rise, nearly invisible in its lush surroundings of cedar, jacaranda, bottlebrush and wisteria, didn't seem to have a front, only a backside it presented on all sides, as self-effacing as though it wished to be forgotten. The pose must have worked, for the house had stood, or squatted, for over 400 years.

Esaías dismounted, dropped La Gata's reins on the ground, and took out a curiously shaped brass key he carried in his waistcoat. Unlocking a small wooden gate in the wall, he struggled to pull it outward against the unchecked growth.

Within the enclosure was a miniature garden almost gemlike in its perfection. Low boxwood hedges hugged the wall on two sides, filling the air with their pungent odor. A veranda, or portico, flanked the other two sides along the house. Next to the portico grew blood red roses, almost funereal in their intensity of color. Huge pots of fuschias hung from the protruding vigas of the portico, catching the sun and contrasting sharply with the deep shade against the house.

At the center of the garden, a fountain as squat as the house itself gurgled softly; the cold spring water spilled over its thick, green-stained lips and ran obediently along channels in the flagstone paving to form a shining ribbon that laced the garden in severe Moorish symmetry before disappearing under the hedges. The fountain had run steadily since the house was built, the springs within the earth seemingly inexhaustible.

Esaías walked along the wooden portico to a small door and knocked. This was his father's study, and only the old man had a key to this door. After a moment, the door swung slowly inward, leaving Esaías straining to see into the gloom of the interior before stooping to enter the doorway. His father was already reseated behind his massive desk, as though the door had opened of its own volition.

The small, sallow-skinned man sat regarding his second son with large unblinking eyes like some nocturnal creature.

Esaías always felt awkward in this study, large and clumsy among the fragile books and stacks of tissue-thin papers that would crumble to dust in a good gust of wind.

Here lay his father's treasure. Here were his books, accumulated one at a time, sometimes a few pages at a time, smuggled in saddle bags surrounding preserved foods, or wrapping a trinket from overseas. It had taken thirteen generations to compile this library, thirteen generations since all things Jewish, all signs of learning and Hebraic study had been burned by the townspeople of Saltillo, since Esaías' forebearers had gained the lives of their wives and children by changing their names and agreeing to be baptized into the Holy Roman Church.

A special branch of the Inquisition had been imported directly from Spain, like any other luxury not afforded by the New World, for the purpose of eradicating an outbreak of heresy in this colonial outpost. It had been made unbearably odious by the fact that several families of Semitic heritage held appointed posts within the provincial government, owned rich farmland, and had some of the finest homes to be seen. A group of merchants had written to the Papal Nuncio in Mexico City and demanded that these affronts to their faith and their pocketbooks be rectified. The Governor of the Province had been roasted alive in a dry cauldron for admitting that he was a Jew.

Esaías' father was named Julio Vargas Caravál. Esaías was the first son in thirteen generations to bear an overtly Jewish name, a name whispered from generation to generation, written on a scrap of parchment and pressed furtively into the unsuspecting palm of a boy on the verge of adulthood, accompanied by the revelation: "I have something important to tell you, my son. You are a Jew."

Esaías' full name had been written in the parish register, Esaías Carabajal de Vargas y Armadio, a Biblical name, a good name, but one which caused the priest to pause and look more carefully at Julio Vargas Caravál and Mariana Armadio Vargas before pursing his lips, blotting the excess ink from the page and closing the sacred tome with heavy finality. It was done. Esaías was named after the unhappy Governor Carabajal who had lost his skin, then his life in 1596 after publicly declaring that, were it not for the Inquisition, there would be fewer Christians in this kingdom than he could count on the fingers of his hands.

Esaías stood in this dark, crowded room, hemmed in by precariously balanced stacks of books, half-empty inkwells, broken quills. He stood too tall, his shoulders hunched under the weight of thirteen generations, under the name he bore, pinned against the six-inch-thick door at his back by his father's unblinking gaze. Esaías had no love of books, of tradition, or of enclosed places. He had come to tell his father goodbye.

Julio Vargas had, of course, already heard of his son's situation.

"This gold business," he said, "it is an addiction, like whiskey or gambling. No one in my family has ever had an addiction before."

Esaías looked around the crowded room and shrugged. "What do you call this?" he asked.

Julio was taken aback. "I call this the word of God."

"God lives in many places," said Esaías, "not just in this room." He was astonished at his own outspokenness. He had never before addressed his father in this manner.

His father regarded Esaías for several more moments.

"You have a beautiful wife," he finally said, "and beautiful children. Miguelito will be a scholar, even if you're not. Try not to lose them."

For this, Esaías had no answer. Unable to meet his father's eyes again, he took his leave.

The old man sat in the darkened room and pondered this wild stranger who was his son. He recalled Moses' parting words to the People of Israel shortly before they entered the Promised Land. God had offered both a blessing and a curse: that the People would be led to a strange land, far beyond their knowledge, where they would worship gods of wood and of stone. The sky would be like copper, and the ground below them like iron. That part had been meant as a curse, but Esaías pursued the minerals in the hills as though they were the Holy Grail, the Seven Cities of Cíbola, the Burning Bush.

A bag of silver and a bag of gold. Esaías touched his saddlebags where the precious metal was carefully stored. This time he also carried a petaca, a leather trunk behind his saddle, with a few of his worldly possessions. He stopped on the low rise north of Saltillo, where he could catch a last glimpse of the spacious streets, the generous houses, and the spreading branches of the well-tended gardens. Home. Or was it his home anymore? He was too confused to know.

Over his shoulder stretched wilderness, ragged hills running north to the Texas border, outlaws and cold nights and shining bits of metal reflected in limpid water. Perhaps that's what the salamander meant, he mused. One man, two worlds.

The image of shining water continued to fill his head, rushing swiftly, wearing away the black soil and rock accumulated over generations to reveal the heart of gold beneath.

Esaías spurred his horse and turned her towards the setting sun with a series of low, short whistles.

"Go!" he said. "La Esmeralda is waiting for us."

◇ ◇ ◇

A sudden flight of birds or movement of wind made Estela stop and gaze out the window. She could not say why, but she felt a lightness she had not felt in many years.

She should feel terrible, thought Estela. Left alone to cope with the household by herself—her surly father, the prying neighbors—an abandoned woman. Estela tried to feel sorry for herself, something she had done often enough before, but today she could not.

The last flowers of the season were still blooming. Her daughters played in the courtyard, their embroidery in a careless heap on a table. Miguelito read in a corner of the patio, his feet up, sweet tea at hand. My little man, she thought.

Esaías was gone again, but this time she had done something about it. Perhaps that was the difference.

Leaving the kitchen, Estela wiped her hands on her apron and pulled it off over her head. She walked into the parlor and opened its wide windows onto the sunny yard. Normally reserved for guests, the parlor stood unused most of the time. Estela picked a book of verse out of a shelf, sat down in the most comfortable chair facing the window, and decided to read until it got too dark.

Somewhere, a cock crowed, a horse whinnied, a cry of elote, elote, roasted corn, floated on the evening breeze. She smelled sewage for a moment, followed by orange blossoms.

Oh wretched moment of my birth, said the first verse she read,

When I opened eyes that one day would gaze upon you,
That one day would see the hand that never would be mine
Eyes that would see you speak the name of another,
See your lips tremble on that name...

Normally, Estela would find her heart beating rapidly when she read such things, but today the words were full of air. A pleasant light came in from the west-facing window, bathing her in its golden glow. Soon it would be too cool to enjoy the evenings like this. A light wind lifted the leaves of the trees, the wind from the mountains that blew everything clean, cleansing the air of the town of the eternal dust of the desert.

ABOUT THE AUTHOR

Kathleen Alcalá lives in Seattle, Washington, with her husband and young son. She is an Assistant Editor with *The Seattle Review* and Co-editor and co-founder of *The Raven Chronicles*, begun in 1991.

Ms. Alcalá has an M.A. in English from the University of Washington, where she was a 1984 Milliman Scholar in Creative Writing, and a B.A. in Human Language from Stanford University.

Selected Titles from Award-Winning CALYX Books

Killing Color, by Charlotte Watson Sherman.
Compelling, otherworldly stories that explore the African American experience. "Lyrical and mesmerizing..." — Publishers Weekly
ISBN 0-934971-17-X, $8.95, paper; ISBN 0-934971-18-8, $16.95, cloth.

Black Candle: Poems about Women from India, Pakistan, and Bangladesh, by Chitra Divakaruni.
A stunning poetry collection that celebrates the passion and the pain in the lives of women from South Asia.
ISBN 0-934971-23-4, $8.95, paper; ISBN 0-934971-24-2, $16.95, cloth.

Ginseng and Other Tales from Manila, by Marianne Villanueva.
Poignant short stories set in the Philippines.
ISBN 0-934971-19-6, $8.95, paper; ISBN 0-934971-20-X, $16.95, cloth.

Idleness Is the Root of All Love, by Christa Reinig, translated by Ilze Mueller. These poems by the prize-winning German poet take two older lesbians through a year together in love and struggle.
ISBN 0-934971-21-8, $10, paper; ISBN 0-934971-22-6, $18.95, cloth.

The Forbidden Stitch: An Asian American Women's Anthology, edited by Shirley Geok-lin Lim, et. al. The first Asian American women's anthology. **Winner of the 1990 American Book Award.**
ISBN 0-934971-04-8, $16.95, paper; ISBN 0-934971-10-2, $29.95, cloth.

Women and Aging, An Anthology by Women, edited by Jo Alexander, et. al. The only anthology that addresses ageism from a feminist perspective. A rich collection of older women's voices.
ISBN 0-934971-00-5, $15.95, paper; ISBN 0-934971-07-2, $28.95, cloth.

In China with Harpo and Karl, by Sibyl James. Essays revealing a feminist poet's experiences while teaching in Shanghai, People's Republic of China.
ISBN 0-934971-15-3, $9.95, paper; ISBN 0-934971-16-1, $17.95, cloth.

Indian Singing in 20th Century America, by Gail Tremblay. A work of hope by a Native American poet.
ISBN 0-934971-13-7, $8.95, paper; ISBN 0-934971-14-5, $16.95, cloth.

Forthcoming

The Nicaraguan Women Poets Anthology, edited by Daisy Zamora. A collection of poetry by Nicaraguan women—Miskito Indian women, early 20th century poets, and better-known poets writing since the 1960s.
ISBN 0-934971-27-7, paper; ISBN 0-934971-28-5, cloth. Prices pending.

Open Heart, by Judith Sornberger. Poetry that explores the experience of growing up in the plains of Nebraska, uncovering what it means to be a woman in Western culture. The author describes her work as "a kind of archaeology, a search for meaning in my own life by identifying and seeking to know intimately my ancestors, both real and imagined."
ISBN 0-934971-31-5, paper; ISBN 0-934971-32-3, cloth. Prices pending.

CALYX Books is committed to producing books of literary, social, and feminist integrity.

CALYX, A Journal of Art and Literature by Women

Celebrating 16 years of publishing the finest of women's creativity! The twice-yearly CALYX Journal combines poetry, fiction, essays, reviews, and art in a beautiful format to bring you the work of women writers and artists from around the world.

These books and the CALYX Journal are available at your local bookstore or direct from:

CALYX, PO Box B, Corvallis, OR 97339

(Please include payment with your order. For book orders, add $1.50 postage for first book and $.75 for each additional book.)

CALYX, Inc., is a nonprofit organization with a 501(C)(3) status. All donations are tax deductible.

Colophon

The text type is set in Goudy. Titles are in Belwe condensed.
Page composition and design by
ImPrint Services, Corvallis, Oregon.